LIP LOCKS & BLOCKED SHOTS

HEATHER C. MYERS

Chapter 1

SERAPHINA HANSON WAS NOT LOOKING FORWARD to going to Las Vegas this weekend. It was Wednesday – the day after Valentine's Day – and her phone buzzed with a reminder to check on the status of her flight. Despite the fact that her grandfather – well, technically her and her older sister Katella – owned a private jet and could schedule things whenever they wanted, Seraphina liked to schedule things accordingly.

She had completely forgotten about the game this Saturday against the Las Vegas Blackjacks, a new hockey team that became part of the National Hockey League that was voted on last year. An expansion draft took place this past summer – which was how she lost Ben Avery, her star defenseman – and they started playing officially this season. This was the first game the Newport Beach Seagulls would play the Las Vegas Black-jacks and as general manager and owner of the team, she wanted to play nice. It was out of the norm for her to attend away games – in fact, this was her first away game she attended this season.

Her head was already throbbing thanks to the fact that she still had to go shopping for a nice gown. Apparently, the Vegas team manager wanted to take her out to dinner before the game and show her around the strip. She wasn't sure she actually wanted to do that but he was doing it for all GMs and she didn't want to be perceived as snotty — on top of all the other negative traits she was known for — by the media. Being the only female GM meant she had to play by their rules. For now.

At that moment, Katella Hanson bounded into her office without even thinking of knocking, a big smile on her face.

"Sera!" she sing-songed, her green-gold eyes shining when she saw her sister sitting behind her desk. "It's almost here! Why are you looking like that? You look like you're holding in a fart."

Seraphina shot her sister a look. "Gross," she said. "Does Negan like when you talk like that?"

Katella snorted and took a seat across from her. "You should hear what Negan says," she pointed out. "Plus, I never use the word fart in front of him. That word doesn't exist in my vocabulary when he's around. It's still new."

James Negan was a second-line center and Katella's boyfriend. Seraphina was actually surprised when the two got together just because they constantly went at it with each other whenever they were in the same room. However, Seraphina knew Katella had gone through a lot and if Negan made her happy, Seraphina would support the two. Plus, to be honest, Seraphina hadn't known anyone else to take care of Katella, to really care about her, the way Negan did for Katella. And Katella had dated third-line center Matt Peters for a couple of years prior.

Seraphina had thought Matt was it for her sister. The One. They seemed happy, maybe not as physically affectionate but Seraphina always thought that was because they felt uncomfortable due to the fact that he was a player and she was his boss's daughter and didn't want to flaunt their relationship. But once her grandfather died, Matt got weird. He pulled away and they wound up breaking up a few weeks after the funeral. He demanded to be traded so Seraphina traded him to Buffalo in exchange for a couple of draft picks. After her first season, Matt's one-year contract expired and as an unrestricted free agent, any team had the opportunity to sign him. No one did. As such, he requested to train with the Gulls over the summer and Seraphina gave him a roster spot just before the season, signing him to a one-year contract as a third-line center. It was purely a business decision but Katella was a mess earlier this year. She hooked up with a fourth-line winger and goon, Xander Vane, and they fizzled out after a few weeks. At least they were both professional about it and both parties involved knew they were just having fun for the time being. Then Katella and Matt had some issues and it didn't help when somehow Negan got involved but luckily, everything settled down and it looked as though everything was fine. Everyone was happy. And the team didn't have any issues.

"So," Katella drawled, perking her eyebrows. "How's everything on the Thorpe front? Getting anywhere with that?"

Seraphina grunted. "Of course not, Kat," she said, picking her eyes up from all the paperwork she wanted to complete. "He is my star goalie, the captain of the team. How can I get anywhere with him if I'm not allowed to date him?"

"You're the boss, Sera," Katella pointed out. "You get to make that call, not anyone else. Plus, no one has to know about you guys even being together. I learned from Matt and even Xander that I don't need everyone to know my business. It's not that I'm ashamed of Negan but it sucks when people call you names. I don't need that and I'm sure Negan doesn't need that, either. Although, I think he kind of ruined that when he fought Guzman a couple of weeks ago."

Seraphina nodded, pressing her lips together as if to say *I told you so*. "I remember that fight," she said. "Wasn't Guzman trying to get a reaction out of Matt?"

"Yeah," Katella said. "Negan reacted instead. Practically threw the gloves off. Almost damaged his hands because Guzman wears a shield." She shook her head, the corners of her lips tilting up. "At least I know I can count on him to have my back."

Seraphina snorted.

"Anyway," Katella continued. "We're not here to talk about me. We're here to talk about you."

"Actually," Seraphina said, standing up. "We're here to go shopping since you're telling me my business clothes aren't good enough for Vegas."

"True," Katella says with a nod. "I'm glad you understand."

The two drove down PCH to Fashion Island, an outdoor mall catered to the affluent population on Newport Beach. There were a lot more boutiques at the mall - along with department stores including Nordstroms and Macy's, Victoria's Secret and Barnes & Noble - as well as a food court that had recognizable restaurants along with some trendy cafes. There were koi ponds and fountains throughout the mall and there was a sense in the air that this mall was much more exclusive than even the Spectrum in Irvine or The Mission Viejo mall further south.

The sisters preferred Fashion Island just because this was the mall they were used to since they grew up here, unless they wanted to see a movie. Then, they typically visited the Spectrum just because the movie theatre had 21 theatres and was huge.

Katella drove - Katella loved to drive and Seraphina loved that her sister loved to drive since it meant she didn't have to. Technically, she could hire a driver and have him drive her around but she didn't want to be a lazy rich asshole if she could help it. Her grandfather had always been hands-on. He worked hard, made the right investments - property rather than stocks - and built up his wealth by saving, living well under his means. He was the epitome of discipline and Seraphina tried to emulate his value as best as she could. It was a way for her to keep his memory alive and, hopefully, do justice to his legacy. It was why he owned the team and partook in general manager responsibilities. He hired scouts and he had someone he trusted to discuss negotiations regarding movement and trades when he couldn't do it himself.

Seraphina had huge shoes to fill, especially considering she had no idea what he was doing. Since the team stemmed from his wealth, her grandfather hadn't formed a board to do what was best for the company. He did hire a good coach - who took Seraphina under his wing and taught her as much as he could. Every now and then, she would bring Henry Wayne in for a consult as well, just to put certain things in terms she could understand. She still had a long way to go, and she knew that, but she was doing her own research and talking to those that would help her. She was learning as much as possible.

Which made it hard to date at all, much less one of her own players.

"So," Katella drawled. "Tell me about you and Brandon. I thought the last time we talked you were going to make a move on him finally."

"I thought so too," Seraphina said with a nod of her head. Her eyes were in her lap as Katella pulled out of the parking lot. She sunk into the familiar cushion of the dark leather seats and glanced out the window. She loved that her grandfather decided to put the Ice Palace on PCH, right across the street from the beach. She loved being able to look out her window and watch the sun glittering against the water. It calmed her down and reminded her that her grandfather's memory was still alive in her, that he was with her even when she felt so, so alone. "But I didn't, I haven't. I'm just... I don't know, Kat. I'm not you. I don't have this confidence where I can talk to a guy the way you can talk to a guy. Plus, I'm his boss and I know I make the rules but still. Think about it. We start dating and St. Louis wants to trade for him."

Katella snorted. "Yeah, right," she said. "You would never trade Thorpe, even if you weren't dating. I know he's a goalie and it's risky but have you considered a long-term contract with him? I mean, instead of six or seven-year deals like some big-name forwards have, you could do three or four. It would prevent him from going anywhere else, although, if I'm being honest, he wouldn't go anywhere else, even if the deal was fucking good."

"What makes you say that?" Seraphina asked, ripping her eyes away from the beach to look at her sister.

Katella rolled her eyes and shot her sister a quick look before resuming her concentration on the road ahead of her. "Sera, I don't get how you could be the dumbest smart person I know," she said. "Thorpe is in love with you. He doesn't talk like it at all but it's so obvious." Seraphina felt her cheeks start to turn pink. "And don't pretend like you aren't aware of this. I've been telling you he's in love with you for forever so don't play dumb."

Seraphina rolled her eyes at her sister's contradiction but didn't say anything. Instead, she let her thoughts drift to Thorpe and what it might be like to actually date him. He would hold her hand, she would lean her head on his chest.

"Are you even listening to me?" Katella asked as they pulled into the parking lot just outside of Macy's. Even though it was lunch time during the week, the parking lot was nearly full. "Look, we have to get you an amazing dress so when Thorpe sees you in it, his jaw drops."

Seraphina rolled her eyes but didn't dismiss the idea. And if her dress caused a reaction in Thorpe, all the better.

Chapter 2

ONCE THE SHOPPING business was done with for the day, Seraphina returned to work to finish all the necessary paperwork she needed to complete before she – along with the team – left the next day. Katella didn't understand why Seraphina just didn't take the rest of the day off but, truth be told, Seraphina wanted to focus her nervous energy on something she was good at. And she was good at paperwork and budgets and now, after a lot of practice, team stats. She also had an article to proof for the Gulls blogger, Harper Crawford, who would also be joining them on the trip to Vegas and was currently dating first line center, Zachary Ryan.

It took everything in Seraphina not to reach out to her friend and get advice about how she managed to date somebody she worked with. How did they balance business and pleasure? Granted, it was a little different since both Zachary and Harper were both employees. Seraphina was the boss, which meant if she did date anyone in the organization, it might come off as untoward.

Especially if that someone was a Gulls player.

Her cheeks turned pink just thinking about Brandon Thorpe

and she had to shake her head and take a cold drink of water. She had had a thing for him for nearly a year and she had yet to do anything about it. She was chickenshit and she knew it.

The truth of the matter was, she was worried how people would perceive her. When she first inherited the team, it was surrounded by the scandal that came from her grandfather's murder. When she was announced as the new manager and owner, she was ripped to pieces by the media. Everything was on the chopping block, from her hair to her clothing to her dismal debut season. Sometimes, they took pictures of her watching the games at the Newport Ice Palace and would deign to write comments about what she was thinking when, the truth of the matter was, she bit into a cold hot dog. She could never win.

If it came out that she was dating her star goalie and captain of the Newport Beach Seagulls – also a former suspect in her grandfather's murder – she would be ripped to shreds. In fact, she didn't know if it was allowed for her to date him. Although, since the Gulls was her team, it would make sense that she got to make her own rules.

Regardless, they would never take her seriously as a legitimate GM and owner.

"Hey."

Her head snapped up and the man that currently stained her thoughts stared at her from her doorway. Brandon Thorpe stared at Seraphina with piercing pale green eyes and a curious look on his face. He never ceased to take her breath away. He wasn't typically handsome – his chin was maybe too big but that was all she could really think of. He had whiskers on the lower half of his face and sharp cheekbones, his short, brown hair disheveled.

He was six feet one, one hundred and ninety-one pounds of solid muscle. She knew that from his stats. He also had a .093 save average which was amazing and, if everything went well, should qualify him for the Vezina Trophy at the NHL Awards in

Vegas later in the summer, once the season wrapped up. If anyone deserved it, it was Thorpe.

Currently, he was wearing a heather-grey crew-cut shirt with the navy blue anchor and Seagulls scrawled in the familiar text they used on the majority of their products. He had fitted dark blue jeans and tennis shoes on his feet. Not the snazziest dresser, either. But still, he left her in awe.

"Hey," she managed to finally say. She had no idea why, but she was more comfortable talking to other GMs regarding trades than she was talking to Brandon Thorpe. Yet, at the same time, he also had this ability to make her feel safe and comfortable. Like she could be herself and not get judged by her flaws. And Seraphina knew she had a number of those.

"I wanted to talk to you about that trip," he said in his low voice. He was born in Ontario so he still had a hint of lilt to it. "We leave tomorrow at eight am, correct?" He perked his brow, making him look younger than his thirty years. Almost boyish, in fact. Downright beautiful, either way.

"Sure," she said, gathering up her paperwork and evening them out by hitting them on the surface of her desk. "Please." She gestured at an empty seat in front of her before placing the pages in her top drawer – a place for them to be only temporarily and to make her desk appear cleaner than it really was. "Sit."

He gave her a small smile, amused by her clear awkwardness, and took a seat in front of her. His tall, lean frame made the chair look small and insignificant.

"So," she said, breathless. Why was she breathless? She hadn't even moved in the past couple of hours, except to go shopping. She shouldn't be breathless now, in front of Brandon. *Control yourself, girl!* "What's up?"

"The guys wanted to know if there were any obligations they needed to be aware of while we're in Vegas," he said. "I know there's that dinner-"

"No." Seraphina shook her head. "Wait, you mean with Phil Bambridge? No, that's just with me."

"Just with… you?" he asked, each word enunciated carefully. "So Katella isn't going either?"

Seraphina shook her head. "No," she said. "It'll just be me and Phil." She caught sight of the look on his face and tilted her head to the side. "Why, though? What's wrong?"

"Nothing's wrong," Brandon replied quickly. "Why would you think something's wrong?"

"Your eyes get green like the grass when you're thinking about something and you're trying to figure out how to phrase it," she said and then turned red – again – at how much she had just revealed.

"So that's a GM meeting tomorrow night," Brandon said slowly. There was something in his tone, something that indicated he was slightly suspicious of it.

"Yes," Seraphina drawled, tilting her head to the side and slowly raising an eyebrow. "Is that a problem?"

Brandon furrowed his brow, shaking his head as his arms crossed over his chest. "No," he said. "No, of course not. You do what you need to do in order to… do whatever it is you do…" He shook his head, wincing after he finished his sentence. "That came out weird. I'm sorry. It was just my understanding that this would be a meeting between you guys and the captains. I didn't realize it was going to be just you and him. Like a date."

"A date?" Seraphina shot him a look. "Are you only asking this because I'm a female and he's a male and we're going to dinner?"

Brandon clenched his teeth together and looked away. "I just find it highly suspicious that this guy's been set to be GM of the Blackjacks since last season and it's only now, when we're set to play the team, does he decide he wants to meet with you," he said. Before Seraphina could jump in and explain, he pushed on. "What's your meeting about? The trade deadline is coming up, sure. Are you planning to make some moves?"

"I don't know what it's about," she said, sounding defensive. To be fair, it seemed as though he was interrogating her and she had no idea why that was. "If it was about trades, you know I couldn't tell you, anyway."

Brandon pressed his lips together. He looked like he wanted to argue. He looked like he wanted to say something. But she also knew there was nothing he could say. Even if she was friends with him, even if they were lovers, she would not be able to divulge any information to him, even if she wanted to.

"Listen," she murmured, trying to soften her tone. "What's on your mind?"

He shrugged his shoulder, looking away. She furrowed her brow. She hated when he did this.

To be honest, Seraphina and Brandon hadn't really spoken much. Maybe a few times a month, if that, and always with other people around due to the fact that it was due to a professional question or issue she needed to give a final say on. He hadn't sought her out on his own in a long time. Maybe even since her grandfather's murder investigation. She wouldn't necessarily say they were friends. Technically speaking, she was his boss and he was her player. But she was crazy, stupid in love with him. Whenever Brandon didn't want to answer a question or he got an answer he didn't like, he withdrew. He looked away. He crossed his arms. He pressed his lips together. He stopped talking. And that was saying a lot, considering he didn't talk much in the first place.

"Are you disappointed you're not going to meet with Phil Bambridge?" Seraphina teased, her eyes lighting up with a sparkle. "I can put in a good word for you, if you want. I didn't realize you were so eager to jump ship and head to Vegas."

Brandon cut her a look that caused the smile to slip off of her face. "The last person I would ever want to play for is Phil Bambridge," he said. "The guy's an asshole."

"An asshole?" Seraphina asked, giving him a doubting look. "Isn't that a little strong, Brandon?"

Brandon's brow furrowed so deep, a prominent wrinkle appeared just above his nose. He gave her a jerking look, his pale green eyes flashing emerald.

"Strong?" he asked. "You think that's strong? I think that's being nice about it. Have you done any research on the guy before you agreed to this date?"

"It's not a date," Seraphina insisted. She was starting to get frustrated with his insistence that this was a date when it was definitely not a date and she wouldn't have agreed to it if it was.

"Have any other GMs gone out to dinner with the guy by themselves?" Brandon asked her, quirking a brow.

Seraphina felt her entire body tense. "How am I supposed to know that?" she asked, throwing her arms out and narrowing her eyes. "Do you honestly expect me to ask the guy, hey, have you been taking out every GM who visits your city to dinner or is it just me because if it's just me, I'm not okay with that because it's a date?" She gave him a deadpan look. "Come on, Brandon. If I want to be taken seriously, I can't just assume a meeting is a date. Don't you know how quickly that would be thrown back in my face? Typical female - can't just go to a business dinner without assuming there's more to it." She rolled her eyes for emphasis.

"Okay," Brandon said, his voice tight and controlled. "I understand the predicament you're in-"

"No, you don't," Seraphina said. "Look, I don't mean to interrupt and I'm not saying you can't grasp the concept of what it might be like to be in my shoes. The thing is, you don't actually know what it's like to be a female in a male-dominated profession. It doesn't matter that I have more money than thirty percent of the other owners and that I have arguably the best first line and goal tender in the league. I'm still reading articles about how people think I color my hair or that I wore a skirt that was shorter than my dress from the previous day. No other GM, no other owner, has ever had to go through that. And I get that it's part of the job. Maybe I didn't quite grasp the concept up until I experienced it directly, but I've accepted I'm never going to be taken seriously in the league no matter what I do."

"No, you haven't," Brandon said, shaking his head.

"Excuse me?" Seraphina asked, furrowing her brow.

"You haven't," he repeated. "If you've accepted it, you wouldn't care about your clothes or the way you speak or how your hair is done. Obviously you would look professional, that's not what I'm saying. But you wouldn't worry what people are going to write about. You would do whatever you wanted, regardless. If you want to wear jeans one day or no makeup because you've been here since five in the morning, you do it. If you want to go home in the middle of the day for a nap, you do it. You don't have to live your life based on what you think is expected of you."

"Don't you think I want to do all of those things?" Seraphina asked in a quiet voice. "Don't you think I want to be able to do what every other male GM does? Don't you think I want to make gentlemen's agreements and be trusted to nego- tiate a deal by myself without Henry Wayne stepping in to assist me? Don't you think I want to wear skinny jeans and chucks instead of high-waisted skirts and high heels? Don't you think I'm sick of either straightening or curling my hair because my wavy hair is too messy? Don't you think I want to be with who I want to be with but I can't because that would be ridiculously unprofessional?" She stopped, realizing she had said too much. She clenched her jaw and dropped her eyes to her desk. "Of course I want all of those things, Brandon. But I don't know how to get what I want without sacrificing how the team is perceived. You and I and everybody else represent this organiza- tion. But I hold myself to a higher standard because I'm the owner. I'm the manager."

Brandon clenched his jaw and looked away. "I don't under- stand how Katella can be with Matt Peterson for two years, hook up with Xander Vane, and now be with James Negan, all within the span of a year and you can't wear converse shoes."

He glanced at her. "No offense to your sister, of course, and I wasn't trying to insinuate anything by that but you were both Ken's granddaughters."

"Trust me," she muttered to herself. "I am well-aware about my sisters dating choices and how I cannot make those same choices - not that I would, exactly, but still." Her eyes picked up and locked with his. "You have no idea how badly I want to blow this off, Brandon. Trust me, I do, but-"

"Then blow him off," he insisted, leaving forward and scooting to the edge of his chair. "Bambridge is an asshole and a sleaze ball. Look him up, Seraphina. Look him up and see for yourself. He's been arrested for multiple sexual assault charges and he always bails out and the Vegas DA never decides to prosecute due to little physical evidence. You don't think he'd do the same to you?"

Seraphina furrowed her brow. "I own the Newport Seagulls," she said as though it was the most obvious thing in the world. "If he tried anything, it would be extremely stupid on his part, I have much more money than he does."

Brandon rolled his eyes. "This has nothing to do with money and everything to do with power," he told her. "You, a young female, are equal to him. Even more experienced than him, actually, because you have a season under your belt. You don't think he's threatened by that?"

"Not everyone is threatened by a strong, powerful woman," she pointed out. "You aren't."

"I'm not," he agreed, "but I'm not everyone. And you're more than just strong and powerful, Sera." She shivered when he addressed her by her nickname. He had never done that before. "You're intelligent and passionate and beautiful. Men like Phil Bambridge would rather see you broken."

"You speak as if you know him," Seraphina murmured.

"I know of him," he told her, looking away. "He grew up a couple of neighborhoods down from me in a wealthy family. He knew my sister. I just... I don't want to see anything happen to you."

Seraphina nodded and gave him what she hoped was a reassuring smile. "Thank you for your concern, Brandon," she said, "but I can take care of myself."

Chapter 3

. "I'M LATE!" Katella yelped as she ran down the stairs, her luggage bounding down the carpeted stairs behind her. "I'm so fucking late!"

"Which means we're late!" Seraphina called from the doorway. "Kat, we are only going to be gone three days. It shouldn't be that complicated to figure out what to pack. You used to travel with the team when you were with Matt. I don't understand why it's so complicated now."

Katella returned with her purse slung over her shoulder and her golden blonde hair in disarray. "Okay, yes," she agreed, nodding her head once. "But Matt was... It's just different, Sera. I know this should have been taken care of last night. I just..." She looked away and a small smile lit up her face. Seraphina almost forgot her frustration with her sister seeing Katella genuinely happy. Seraphina couldn't remember a time when Katella looked like this, but she knew it had to be well before her grandfather died, and that was a year and a half ago. "This is my first official trip with Negan. Yeah, I know it's a hockey game so technically he's working and it's not just going to be us and maybe it won't even be that romantic. But this is a big deal and I just want everything to be perfect. We literally got together last month so it's kind of a rush to suddenly take a trip, you know?"

Seraphina pressed her lips together. Unlike her sister, Seraphina didn't have the experience dating hockey players – dating anyone, really. She had had a couple of boyfriends back in high school and even one in college but none that were serious. Not like Katella was already serious with Negan. So she couldn't judge, she couldn't know what Katella was feeling.

But she could be supportive. She could try to understand, even if it meant they were a little late.

"Okay," she said with a gentle nod.

Katella's eyes lit up and she pulled Seraphina in an awkward one-armed hug.

"Thanks," she said. "I think I'm good to go, though. Is Jimmy outside?"

"Jimmy's been outside the past twenty minutes," Seraphina replied. "I actually owe him breakfast now."

Katella snickered as she opened the front door. Jimmy, their driver, rushed up to help the sisters with their minimal luggage before ushering them in the back of the sleek black town car. Seraphina shot one last look at her home, her heart hammering in her chest. She didn't know why, but she had a feeling that this trip was going to change everything.

___

"WELL, WELL, WELL, HANSON," a low, sandpaper voice said as Seraphina and her sister were assisted out of the town car. "Look who decided to show."

Seraphina pressed her lips together and averted her eyes. She knew Negan was referring to Katella rather than her even though their last name was the same.

"Bite me," Katella snapped.

The team, all lined up and dressed in suits, chuckled at the familiar banter. Seraphina watched Negan push his brows high almost as if to say *Don't tempt me, sweetheart.*

Seraphina bit back a smile and kept her mouth shut as she walked past the players and boarded the plane. She knew there was a hierarchy to where the players sat depending on the roles and seniority on the team. However, Seraphina had her preferred seat and since she hated flying in general, she decided her desire won out over some hierarchy. As such, she took a seat in the first row next to the window. She snapped the window cover open and looked out. It was nice to be able to see where they were going and what to expect.

She barely noticed as the team trickled through. She over-heard one of the rookies complain about always having to wear a suit but it was a tradition her grandfather adhered to, even though they didn't have to wear their suits until game day. Regardless, he liked the class it brought to the team and insti-tuted it on travel days as well, which made some players uncom-fortable. The majority went along with it because they respected Ken, and Seraphina kept the tradition as an honor to her grandfather's legacy.

After a moment, someone plopped down next to her. She glanced over, thinking it was her sister, and found herself staring at the chiseled profile of Brandon Thorpe. She immediately snapped her eyes away, not fully believing that this was happening.

"Where's Katella?" she managed to get out. Her tone made it sound like she wasn't pleased by his presence and she shut her eyes, muttering at herself internally for not being careful about how she was presenting particular inquiries. "I'm sorry, that's not what I –" She tried to give him a charming smile and hoped it didn't come out like she didn't want him there. Because she did. At least, she thought she did. Actually, she didn't want him to see her hyperventilate due to her fear of flying. "Never mind. I take it back."

He quirked a brow. "You take what back?" he asked. "The apology or the question itself?"

"Um, the question," Seraphina mumbled. "Sorry. I was just expecting my sister to sit here."

"I can go and get her if you want," Brandon said. "I think Katella found her own row that may or may not include Negan. As captain, I sit up front. And as someone who doesn't socialize, I was expecting to sit alone. But you're here so I figured I would sit next to you."

Seraphina felt her cheeks turn pink. "That's totally fine," she said. "My bad."

He gave her an odd look that included a furrowed brow and a cocked head. Seraphina felt herself sink further into her chair.

"Listen," he said, reaching back to cup the back of his neck. "I just wanted to apologize for yesterday. It wasn't my intention to have you think I didn't take you seriously or that Phil Bambridge didn't take you seriously. I shouldn't have said anything. I just…" He clenched his jaw so it popped and Seraphina's eyes were drawn to the chiseled jawline. "I'm sorry, okay?"

"I feel like this is coming out wrong," Seraphina said. Before she could say more, a pretty flight attendant began to announce the plane would be taking off and to please sit down and fasten seat belts. Seraphina felt her fingers curl around the end of the armrest, her knuckles turning white.

Brandon glanced at her profile. His stare lingered a moment before dropping down to her hands. She hoped he didn't notice how tight her grip was. She hoped he didn't realize that her skin had gone pale. Her seatbelt was already fastened and her seat was upright. Her window was up, the sun already up and seeping through the window. The sunlight warmed Seraphina's face but it didn't do anything to calm down. Her heart was pounding against her chest like the victim of a horror movie locked up in the trunk of a car, pleading to get out.

Without saying a word, Brandon placed his hand over hers.

He didn't even look at her. However, her mouth dropped open and she looked at him with wonder in her eyes, surprised that someone as reserved and as stoic as he was would think to cover her hand with his.

His hand was big and covered hers perfectly. It was callused but warm and while it didn't make the fear disappear the way she wanted it to, it helped relax her just a little. And to her, a little was enough.

"I'm afraid of snakes," Brandon said, breaking the silence. He stared straight ahead but his thumb began to move up and down the back of her hand, so light, like a butterfly's wing. "When I was a kid, my older brother had a pet snake. It got out and somehow ended up in my bed at night. It was just a garden snake but I can still feel the smooth scales against my arm." He shuddered and his eyes snapped closed. "Ever since, I've hated them. I don't go hiking anywhere where there's a chance a snake could be present. Which sounds ridiculous since we live in Southern California."

Seraphina felt her lips curl up and her heart warmed at what he was doing. Talking.

"So you're like Indiana Jones?" Seraphina asked. The two flight attendants began reading instructions on safety, demonstrating with their props as the plane backed out from the gate.

Brandon chuckled, a smile lighting up his face. It momentarily distracted her from her fear and she stared at it as long as possible, despite the fact that she might come across as crazy. She wanted to memorize it.

"I wouldn't go that far," he said. "He is way better looking than me, for starters, plus he has the whip, which I would never be able to manage, and he can pull off a fedora like nobody's business."

Seraphina started laughing, even more of the tension leaving her body, even though the jet was racing down the runway, about to take off at any moment.

"I don't know," Seraphina said with a shrug. "You're kind of a badass in front of the net. You know how some players have an incredibly hard shot goaltenders are afraid to stand in front of them. I feel like some shooters are afraid to shoot when you're in front of net."

Brandon threw his head back and started laughing. It wasn't even that funny but her tone was awkward and it was almost a ridiculous thing to say in the first place.

Seraphina reveled in the sound. It was like music to her ears and she was so proud to be the one who caused it. She wanted to make him laugh always.

"I'm serious, Brandon," she told him, her eyes catching his. "Regardless of where we end up in the playoffs, if we make the playoffs, you're going to get nominated for the Vezina. And if you don't win it..." She shook her head. "Well, we all know the hockey media is biased to the east coast, but still."

He shrugged his shoulders and looked away. He was uncomfortable with flattery, uncomfortable with being honored for something he loved to do. He hadn't told her that, but she picked up on it. Last season, even though they played horribly, talk began about Thorpe possibly getting nominated for the Vezina, but that died down just as quickly as it started. There was no way the NHL was going to award a goaltender whose team didn't even make playoffs.

"Did you always want to play goalie?" Seraphina pushed. She knew it was asking a lot, to try and get him to talk more when he didn't talk much at all, but she found she liked hearing the sound of his voice. She liked that he was comfortable enough with her to share these parts of him not many people knew.

Brandon nodded his head. "My older sister Cameron played hockey and liked using me to practice, even when I was really young," he explained. "It freaked my mom out but my dad said it was a good way for me to toughen up. I mean, I was five and my sister was shooting pucks at me. I didn't have any gear except one of her own hockey helmets and a lot of layers of clothing."

"Your sister was the woman at the auction, right?" Seraphina asked.

Brandon nodded, rolling his eyes as a smile tugged at the corner of his lips.

"That's Rachel for you," he said with a shrug of his shoulders. "We haven't seen each other in a few months so she decided to surprise me by attending the auction without even telling me. She does well for herself back home - she's an accountant - but she hasn't settled down yet. She likes her freedom so I suppose she's waiting for the right person."

"She sounds like she's not waiting at all," Seraphina murmured.

The plane took off into the sky at a steep angle, causing her to grip the hand rests tighter once more. Brandon didn't tighten his grip on her but he didn't remove his hand, either. Instead, he kept it over her hand, tracing mindless patterns into her skin, trying to distract her in any way he could.

"What do you mean?" he asked, looking over at her. He had to raise his voice just a bit to be heard over the noise.

Seraphina swallowed, trying to pull herself out of her funk and focus on his touch, on his voice.

"Your sister," she finally said. "She doesn't sound like she's the type of woman to wait around for the right guy. I don't think she's waiting around at all. She's going after what she wants. She has a good job, she sounds like she'd be the type to have lots of friends, and she still makes an effort to not lose touch with her baby brother. Romance seems like the last thing on her mind. She sounds amazing."

Brandon was silent for a long moment, letting Seraphina's words sink in. Then, he turned to her and murmured, "She said the same thing about you."

"Me?" Seraphina asked as the plane leveled out. Her eyes were wide. "She knows about me?"

"I've mentioned you from time to time," he said, not meeting her eyes. "I wanted to introduce you to her that night but then the whole drama between Peters and Negan occurred and I didn't think that was the right time. But from what she knows of you, she likes you. But she won't make her final decision until she meets you herself."

"I look forward to meeting her," Seraphina murmured, the tips of her cheeks turning red.

The plane ride was still tense thanks to Seraphina's constant discomfort for flying. But it was a lot more bearable thanks to Brandon being next to her and holding her hand.

Chapter 4

SERAPHINA DIDN'T HAVE much time once they arrived at the Vegas airport, took a private bus to their hotel, and checked into said hotel before she had to start getting ready for dinner with Phil Bambridge. There was a nice welcome basket filled with game cards, casino chips, wristbands, as well as snacks and champagne that greeted the two sisters as they made their way into the suite. The players had regular rooms on the east side of The Desert Hotel, a hotel off the strip, two miles from the arena. It was a luxury hotel, with a portion of suites (all rooms in the west building) and a portion of regular rooms. Each player had a roommate and would be staying in a regular hotel in the west tower. Even Harper would be rooming with Seraphina and Katella rather than her boyfriend Zachary Ryan.

Well, Seraphina thought to herself with amusement. *We'll see if that lasts.*

She couldn't help but smirk to herself as she took a long, luxurious shower in the big shower with a stainless steel shower head and divine water pressure. Seraphina wondered if Phil would understand if she just stayed in her shower the whole night and order room service rather than go out to a fancy dinner where nothing tasted good.

However, when Katella started pounding on the door, demanding Seraphina get out so she could use the restroom because the team was going to go out and she wanted to make sure she had enough time to look good, Seraphina knew that probably wouldn't sit well with the manager. She wanted to throw the very fluffy pillow on her bed at her sister. Katella was drop-dead gorgeous and if Negan didn't see that – Seraphina didn't understand how he couldn't but she had heard of weirder things – then he wasn't worthy of Katella in the first place.

Also, Seraphina needed the bathroom more than anyone. She had an important business meeting, not a date.

"I know you're trying to avoid tonight," Katella called through the off-white door. "Nice try!"

Seraphina clenched her jaw and glared at the door. She hated when her sister could read her better than she could read herself. After another moment, she threw open the door only to see Katella half naked, ready to hop in the shower.

"Hope you like cold showers, sis," Seraphina said with a smirk.

"You bitch," Katella muttered but slammed the door shut once she was inside.

Seraphina could hear Harper snickering on her bed.

"What?" Seraphina asked, her lips curling up into a smirk. "You're not going out tonight?"

"Oh, I am," Harper said. "I just don't need the frivolities that others do in order to look good."

"I heard that," Katella called from the bathroom.

"Well, I said it loudly," Harper called back. She glanced over at the fourth bed in their suite. "When does Emma's flight get in?"

"Maybe an hour?" Seraphina replied. "Her rehearsal ended an hour ago and I think her flight's already taken off. Is Kyle picking her up?"

"I heard she's going to Uber it," Harper replied. "I'm sure he wants to, especially with a beautiful girl like Emma coming to Vegas by herself, but she didn't want him to miss out on time with the guys so she's going to meet us here."

Seraphina shook her head. "The things we do for love," she said.

"Or don't do," Harper added innocently.

"And what is that supposed to mean?" Seraphina asked, raising a brow at the golden-haired beauty, typing away on her laptop. If Seraphina had to guess, Harper was trying to finish her article before they went out so she wouldn't have to worry about it for the rest of their time here. There were a few details she would have to add later - game stats and the like - but she was intelligent enough to know how to put a good article together in less than an hour. It was one of the reasons why Seraphina had hired her full-time in the first place.

Harper shrugged innocently, her fingers flying over the keyboard. "Nothing," she said without looking up. "You know, I did see you sitting next to Brandon Thorpe during the flight. How was that?"

"It was pleasant," Seraphina said, turning her back on Harper so Harper couldn't read her flushing face. She hadn't thought anyone had noticed her and Brandon together but now she realized that that was a foolish presumption.

"I'm sure."

Seraphina could hear the smirk in Harper's voice and she tried not to react in order to make it appear that what Harper and Katella were saying didn't affect her in any way. She grabbed the white gown Katella had all but forced her to get. It was the only gown she tried on even though Katella had at least seven more in her arms when they stumbled across this one. When they both saw it, they fell in love with it. It fit beautifully as though it was made specifically for her. When she saw herself in it, she knew that this was it.

26

It was a simple white gown that reached last her ankles but didn't hit the floor if she wore high enough heels. The dress was similar to a Greek goddess toga-dress, held together by thin straps. There was a fair amount of cleavage, the cut being sweetheart. It hugged every curve from the narrow waist to her curvy hips before splitting down her right thigh into two pieces, exposing a fair amount of skin.

She decided to blow dry her hair and then straighten the locks. She put some cream in her hair in order to protect it from all the styling. Once she was done, Katella emerged from the shower in her simple red dress, looking nothing short of stunning and confident. Seraphina wished she had a fraction of Katella a confidence.

"You should pin your bangs back," her sister suggested, coming to stand behind Seraphina and gently brushing her hair. "I have a couple of bobby pins."

Katella disappeared before coming back and did her sister's hair in less than five minutes. "Typically, I hate hairspray but we need your flyaways to be controlled," she said. She spritzed on a decent amount before tilting her head and looking at Seraphina's face. "Now, for your makeup..."

Katella did her makeup and Seraphina was pleasantly surprised that it wasn't over the top. She especially loved the pink lipstick even though she wasn't much of a lipstick person.

By the time Katella was finished, Seraphina was dressed beautifully. She stared at herself in the mirror, going over her reflection with a critical eye. For the past couple of years, there would be B-list celebrities who would attend a Gulls charity event like the woman from an interior design show and the latest Bachelorette. Somehow, the women would be stunning. Drop-dead gorgeous. Flawless. And even though Seraphina knew she, too, was beautiful in her own right, she also felt she couldn't match the perfection and effort these women put into their appearance.

Now, as she stared at herself in the mirror, she realized that this was what it must feel like being one of those women who always had to look good in front of a camera.

She just wished she could have looked like this for a different occasion with a different person.

"What is it?" Katella asked, furrowing her brow as she stared at her sister's reflection in the mirror. "Why do you look like that?"

"Why do you think Brandon Thorpe would call Phil Bambridge an asshole?" she asked in a small voice. She hadn't mentioned her conversation with Brandon to her sister, originally planning to discuss it on the plane. But when Katella didn't sit with her, she didn't have the chance to. Now, however, these feelings were forcing words to come out of her mouth without her full understanding or consent.

Katella raised an eyebrow and her lips curled up into a smirk. "When did this happen?" she asked.

Harper set her laptop to the side of her bed before hurrying over to get in on the conversation. Seraphina had no idea why Harper hadn't started to get ready. Then again, Harper had never been much of a club person. Katella told her that when Harper had picked her up from Taboo, a nightclub in Costa Mesa, she was in a plaid shirt and converse shoes. It wouldn't surprise Seraphina if Harper tried to attend tonight in something casual. Then again, Harper always had a knack for cleaning up pretty well, especially if she wanted to knock Zachary Ryan off of his feet. And she typically did.

"After we went shopping and I went back to the office," Seraphina said. "He came in because he assumed the dinner was for GMs and team captains, but when I told him it was just for GMs, he got frustrated. He said Phil Bambridge is a bad guy, that he knew him as an acquaintance back in Ontario. I guess Bambridge knew his sister or something?" She furrowed her brow and shook her head. "Anyway, he kept calling it a date when it's not a date."

Harper pressed her brows up and shot Katella a knowing look. "That sounds suspiciously like jealousy," she pointed out. "What do you think, Kat?"

"I would agree," Katella said. "And I think if Emma were here, she would as well. Why didn't you tell us this sooner? Sera, if I had known, do you know what I would have put together to-"

"How could you possibly assume he's jealous?" Seraphina asked, her tone doubtful. "Come on. He was just being.." Sexist? Misogynistic? Brandon was none of those things. He wasn't even really an Alpha make due to how quiet and brooding he was.

It was one of the reasons why she liked him so much and one of the things that drove her absolutely crazy. He didn't speak unless he felt compelled to, unless he had something he needed to say. He wasn't the sort to talk just to hear his own voice or because he thought of something because he assumed he was an expert and knew more than anyone else. He was arrogant in front of the net, and maybe his reserved attitude left him seeming snobbish, but at least he didn't talk himself into a rut.

However, on the other hand, the fact that he withheld his true feelings, hid himself off from the world, was frustrating. She wished she knew what he was thinking the majority of the time because he liked to keep things to himself. Whether that was because he assumed he was stronger for not unloading his burdens on anyone else or because he didn't want people to know his problems, Seraphina didn't know. In the end, she supposed it didn't matter. All that mattered was that he was going through problems and he wouldn't share those problems with anyone.

"No," Katella said, shaking her head with certainty. "Thorpe was totally jealous if he's calling Phil Bambridge an asshole."

"Especially since this is the most you guys have talked in a while, right?" Harper asked, furrowing her brow. She strode over to the closet and grabbed a silver cocktail dress she had hung up upon their arrival.

Seraphina nodded once before turning away from the mirror. "So if he's jealous," she said, leaning against the edge of the sink before Katella swatted her away from doing that in case she got her dress dirty or stray drops of water on it. "Why doesn't he just tell me that?"

Harper snorted. "No guy is going to admit they're jealous," she said, matter-of-fact. "That would be a total shot to their pride. Zach did the same thing when my crazy ex wouldn't leave me alone."

"And you know Negan did the same thing with Matt," Katella said, raising her eyebrows in order to emphasize her point. "And now, Brandon's doing it with you." She smirked. "This is a good thing, Sera. It basically proves that he likes you."

"He can like me all he wants, but that doesn't mean we can be together," Seraphina muttered, her voice filled with regret. "There are rules-"

"That you put in place and can change," Katella pointed out and then shot her sister a look. "Actually, you're the only one following your rule, you know that? For some reason, your rules don't apply to anyone else except for you because if they did, I sure as hell wouldn't be allowed to date Negan."

Harper emerged from the bathroom, looking flawless with absolutely no effort into her appearance. If she wasn't so sweet, Seraphina might have hated her just a little bit. She hoped Zachary Ryan knew how lucky he was to have her.

"Don't you have to meet Bambridge, like, now?" Harper asked, clicking on her phone so the time flashed up at them.

"Oh." Seraphina pushed her brow up. "I guess I'm late."

Katella smirked as she walked Seraphina to the door. "Don't sound so upset about it," she murmured. "Have fun, okay? And if you need me or you need an excuse to get out, let me know. Call me, okay?"

"I will," Seraphina promised as she disappeared out the door.

Chapter 5

SERAPHINA GLANCED at the dainty watch she wore on her right wrist she inherited from her grandmother after she died. Phil Bambridge was twenty minutes late and she looked like an idiot waiting for him in a white gown with her hair up and out of her face like she was some trophy. She had already seen the team make their way to one of the three nightclubs located in the casino area of the hotel and she did her best to try and avoid them as best as she could. They didn't need to see how ridiculous she looked. It certainly couldn't top how ridiculous she felt.

Once they were out of sight, she came back to keep looking for Bambridge. Katella had googled him just so Seraphina could see what she was dealing with. Besides being a decent-looking guy in his mid-thirties, there was nothing special about him. She actually felt slightly uneasy based on the way he smirked in his picture. It made a shiver slide down her back and she almost called him to call off their meeting tonight.

It was a meeting, right? Not a... date.

Not a date.

"Hey."

Seraphina jumped and a familiar chuckle crawled down her spine and settled on her skin.

"Hey," she said with a smile as her eyes took in Brandon. "You look…" She let her voice trail off, her cheeks turning pink. "Um, right. I thought the team was already at, you know, the clubs. Or wherever you guys are going."

Brandon's smile grew wider with each passing second and every word out of Seraphina's mouth. The problem was, he looked amazing. Sure, it was just a pressed white collared shirt and charcoal slacks that fit him in all the right places, the small amount of stubble gracing the lower half of his face. Also, his brown hair was messy – it was always messy – but God, he looked beautiful.

"Yeah, they already left," he said. "You look…" He pushed his brows up as he took in the sight of her without being skeevy about it. "As well. I'm surprised you're still here, though. Wasn't dinner a half hour ago?"

"Twenty minutes, more or less," Seraphina corrected. "But yes, Bambridge is late. To be honest, I'm kind of hoping he doesn't show up and I can go back to the room."

"You could always come out with us," Brandon pointed out.

"To be honest, I'm surprised you're actually going out," Seraphina said, feeling the discomfort being around Brandon alone start to leave her. "I know you don't typically go out. Not that you're a hermit but-"

He laughed, a genuine sound that forced Seraphina's lips to turn up on their own.

She had heard the sound of his laughter before, most recently on the plane, and she basked in the sound.

"I'm trying to expand my horizons," he said. "Also, Ryan and Negan have been on my case about it all season. I figured Vegas was the perfect to place to go out." He shrugged. "At least it will get them off my back for a little while." He pulled his green eyes from her and glanced around. "Isn't what's-his-name supposed to be here by now? The plan was for you to be gone before we made our appearance on the floor."

Seraphina laughed. "Probably a smart thing," she agreed. Once again, she glanced at the slender wristwatch on her left wrist and shook her head. A small frown tugged her lips down and she couldn't stop herself from rolling her eyes in annoyance. "Yes, he was. If he's not here in five minutes, I'm leaving. I feel like an asshole, standing here and waiting for the last twenty minutes."

"To be honest, I can't believe you wasted twenty minutes on him," Brandon pointed out, pushing his brows up to emphasize his point. "I know how much you hate wasting your time."

Seraphina cocked her head to the side. He knew that about her? She wasn't sure if she should feel flattered or nervous that he paid attention to her when she didn't realize. What else did he pick up on? That she still bit her nails? That she still ate hot cheetos at her desk like she was some kid in elementary school? That she never wore a pair of matching socks?

"You know," he said, sliding his hands into his pockets and glancing at his black loafers before looking up at her. "You should come out with us."

Seraphina felt her heart flutter. It almost sounded like a date but with a bunch of other people. People that she liked. People she knew wouldn't judge her for socializing with her employees.

For a moment, she let herself think about that. About what it would mean if she said yes. They would get into whatever nightclub together. He would offer to buy her drink. She would ask for a wine. He would tease her about drinking wine at a nightclub. Katella would force her on the dance floor even though she hated dancing. Brandon would join their group. But then, the group would start to disappear leaving the two of them alone. He would look at her, she would look at him. And then, then perhaps, if the moment was perfect and the gods were smiling down on them, he might lean towards her, never breaking eye contact and then, and then she would tilt her head up and...

"I can't," she finally said, forcing herself to pull out of this daydream. Her heart wrenched, as if she was physically pulling away from him. "Trust me, I want to but-"

"But somehow you can go out with some guy who's an actual asshole," Brandon said, "but you can't go out with your team. You can't celebrate being in a new city with your team. I just don't understand that, Sera. Wouldn't you rather be with us?"

"Of course I would," she said with a hiss, her eyes narrowed and her body tense. "Of course I would, Brandon. I would love to hang out with the team socially but that would send the wrong message."

"What, that our boss is down to earth and really cool and just a reminder that we play for an excellent organization in the best hockey town out of every place there's a team?" Brandon asked, slight attitude in his voice. The sarcasm dripped like the cubic zirconium did from her chandelier earrings and she felt herself continue to tense under his smartass remarks. "Don't you think other GMs do team bonding activities and events? Not just the charity events but actual events that are exclusive for our organization."

"Brandon," Seraphina said, her eyes flashing a crisp blue, the gold ring around her iris shining brightly, like the sun in the sky. "What do you want from me here? What can I do to make you happy?"

Brandon clenched his jaw and looked away. It looked as though he wanted to say something, like he wanted her to know something, but he was holding back.

And that was when the word vomit continued to spill out of her like a broken sprinkler to the point where she couldn't stop herself if she tried.

"You talk a lot, Brandon, but God forbid it's thrown back at you," she told him in a dark voice, her eyes narrowed. "God forbid you're required to speak. Sure, have an opinion on my choices and decisions. Have an opinion on my thoughts and my values. But when you're asked to share something about yourself, you clam up. You don't want to talk when it's about you. For once, why don't you take your own advice and do what you want without being held back by anyone or anything. Don't worry about the consequences, just do it!"

At that moment, Brandon's eyes snapped back to hers, and without a word, he strode to her. His long legs only needed two steps before he reached her, and then his hand were in her hair, his other cupping her cheek and tilting her head back so he could kiss her deeply.

It took a moment before Seraphina's eyes closed on their own accord and she was leaning into him, kissing back with all she could muster. He was kissing her. He had kissed her, completely on his own and it was magic, glorious, everything she had ever imagined it would be but more.

A long, low whistle pierced the air and Seraphina ripped herself away from Brandon, even though it was the last thing she wanted to do. She gasped for breath but, from the corner of her eye, she saw Brandon straighten and give the whistler a cold, stoic look. He didn't look affected by the kiss at all. Which was crazy because Seraphina could barely stand straight let alone hold herself together the way Brandon was. She had absolutely no idea how he did it.

Maybe he didn't think the kiss was anything special?

That couldn't be it. He specifically said he wanted to kiss her. It just didn't get to the point of being passionate because someone had interrupted them.

And that someone was Phil Bambridge.

Phil Bambridge was six foot, lean and fit. Handsome in a preppy sort of way. He had slicked back brown hair and blue eyes, a chiseled jaw, and high cheekbones. He wore a suit that looked tailor-made and strode through the lobby like he owned the place. And who knew? Perhaps he did.

"Seraphina Hanson," he drawled in a long voice, looking her up and down. "Don't you look like a sight for sore eyes?"

She cleared her throat and averted her eyes, taking a step back from Brandon. If Phil was focused on her, he would be less likely to notice she had just been kissing her star goaltender. If he didn't notice that, it would be... It would be like the kiss hadn't existed. Because no one saw it. Even though it was the most real thing she had felt in years.

However, one look in his eyes and she knew very well that he had seen it. There was a sparkle in his eyes as they roved up and down Seraphina's frame. It was almost as though the kiss had given Phil permission to look at her like she was some kind of piece of meat just for him. Like she would let anyone kiss her. The sad truth of the matter was, she hadn't been kissed in over a year and now that she had, the entire world looked different. More colorful. She had a new pair of eyes. Her sight had somehow transformed. Before, she would have let Phil look at her that way, rolling her eyes internally and dismissing the behavior as what she had to endure being a woman in a man's world.

But now, she didn't feel quite so forgiving.

"Are you ready to go?" he asked, keeping his eyes fixed on her and completely ignoring Brandon standing there, tense and intimidating.

Seraphina turned to Brandon – almost as if she was forcing Bambridge to acknowledge his presence – and gave him a smile. Hopefully, he would understand what it meant – that she would be okay and that she wanted nothing more than to stay with him instead of be anywhere near Bambridge, and Jesus Christ, he was an amazing kisser – before following Bambridge out of the lobby.

Chapter 6

THE RESTAURANT WAS CALLED Casa Marie, a trendy
Mexican place that catered to young couples on the town.
Seraphina felt entirely too dressed up and she wished she hadn't
worn white, considering Mexican had so many spices and salsas
that could potentially stain her dress and she would be devas-
tated if this dress was ruined in any way.

Despite the fact that the silver town car was heated,
Seraphina couldn't get comfortable against the tan leather seats
in the back. When she snapped her seat belt in, Phil laughed,
calling her adorable and cute but insinuating she was an idiot
with the brain of a child. Instead of talking about sports, he
focused on her appearance. He used the word gorgeous three
times and beautiful twice and actually asked if her players had
asked her out yet and how they were able to hold themselves
back from approaching her.

"My players are all professional," she told him, giving him a
piercing stare from where she sat behind the driver. Not that he
realized it, of course. "They would never ask their GM out."

"Well, I wouldn't fall into that category," Phil said, pride
sparkling in his dark eyes. "If I saw you, it didn't matter who you

were or what position of power you were in, I would go after you until I won you over."

"So you wouldn't respect what I said?" Seraphina asked. Perhaps she should have bit her tongue and ignored the remark. She was sure he meant it as a compliment. But she was starting to get annoyed at the fact that she had to be here in the first place, not because she wanted to be, but because she was trying to be professional and laidback and one of the boys. She didn't find it fair that she had to deal with all of that while the male GMs could reject a business dinner without thinking twice.

Maybe Brandon was right. Maybe she was overthinking things and she should just do what she wanted. This meeting tonight wasn't going to affect the team; it was going to make her look good.

"Come on," Phil said with a roll of his eyes. "Girls love it when a guy chases after them. It's part of the fun, it's part of the game. When they say no, they really mean yes."

Seraphina snorted and rolled his eyes. She didn't care that he saw, either. She didn't care that he shot her a look like she was crazy for thinking otherwise.

"That's ridiculous," she told him. "Quite frankly, that's an offensive assumption and it could get you into a lot of trouble, if it hasn't already."

"Whoa, whoa," Phil said, gesturing with his hands that she should calm down. "I didn't realize I had asked my mom out to a sexy dinner tonight."

"Sexy?" Seraphina raised an eyebrow.

"Yes, sexy," Phil said as though it was the obvious thing in the world. "You have looked at yourself in the mirror, right?"

"Listen," Seraphina said, feeling herself shift uncomfortably. "I'm flattered that you're attracted to me but I'm not interested in a relationship, especially not with a GM. I mean, there's a conflict of interest there and-"

"Relationship?" Phil interrupted with a snort. "Jesus, I'm not looking for a relationship. I just want to have fun with you. The same kind of fun you clearly have with Brandon Thorpe." He wiggles his eyebrows at her, his lips curling into a smooth smile, and before Seraphina even knew what was happening, began to slide his hand up her thigh.

Seraphina immediately grabbed his hand and threw it off of her. Her entire body wretched at the touch, her insides screaming their protests. She needed to get out of here. She needed to get away from him. Brandon was right; Phil Bambridge was an asshole and she was too blinded by doing what she thought was the right thing to realize it. Hell, she hadn't even researched him after Brandon tried to warn her yesterday, back in her office. How could she have been so naive? Why holding she trust that Brandon was right?

She needed to get out of here. She needed to get away from Phil.

"What do you think you're doing?" she demanded, flashing her eyes at him.

"Oh, come on, Seraphina," Phil said with a roll of his eyes. "It's not like I grabbed your boobs or your ass. You're making this into a bigger deal than it needs to be."

Without warning, Seraphina reached back and punched him in the face. The crack of her knuckles sent pain down her hand but the sound was as beautiful as a bird singing a song early in the morning. She would deal with the pain later. The look on his face and the cry emitted from Phil's threat was worth it.

"You, bitch!" Phil exclaimed, clutching his face and shooting her narrowed eyes.

"Driver!" Seraphina called. "I want to get out!"

"Fuck, Seraphina, I think you broke my nose!"

"Maybe you should understand what the hell no means," Seraphina snarled, surprising even herself. She hadn't expected to sound so caustic, then again, she hadn't expected to hit a guy or even be assaulted in the back of a car on the way to what was supposed to be a GM meeting.

"You weren't saying no to Brandon fucking Thorpe," he said

as the driver pulled to the side of the road. "You fucking puck slut. Typical female. This is why women shouldn't be in charge of sports teams. You can't control yourselves around successful athletes."

Seraphina punched Phil again, causing him to scream out a groan.

"You're right," she said as she opened the car door. "I can't seem to control myself."

She slid out with her clutch in her hand. She slammed the door shut and looked around. She was still somewhere populated so she wasn't afraid of being alone in an environment she didn't want to be. It would be easy to flag down a cab and head back to the hotel.

But first, she needed to call her sister.

BRANDON COULDN'T RELAX ENOUGH to enjoy himself at the first nightclub he'd been to in a while. He was never into the nightclub scene, preferring to stay at home and either read, swim, or play Final Fantasy. Sure, he was thirty, but sometimes playing an RPG game on his Playstation 4 helped calm him down after a particularly frustrating game. He had beat the game in record time last season. It also helped take his mind off of the fact that he absolutely, one-hundred percent was head over heels for his boss, Seraphina Hanson. He wasn't the sort of guy to believe in love at first sight, but after their initial encounter, he couldn't get her out of his head and suddenly, he didn't notice the pretty girls in the stands, the pretty news anchors who interviewed them for their half-hour sports show. All he could think about was Seraphina and the utter faith she had in him, despite the fact that he had been a suspect in her grandfather's murder.

Of course, she had the same faith in her team, regardless. Zachary Ryan had been arrested early in the season for assaulting an ex-boyfriend of his current girlfriend, Harper Crawford. Brandon didn't know much about what happened but it sounded like the jackass totally deserved it.

Seraphina was just that sort of person. Filled with faith, even in people she didn't know.

Brandon couldn't be like that. He had grown up with a single mom working two jobs to keep a roof over his head and a sister who took care of him instead of socializing with her friends or go out on dates with boys. They had sacrificed everything for him and his dream – a dream that had never really been his, but his sister's. A dream that she shared with him willingly and without bitterness or jealousy. He owed everything to his family.

But that focus and determination to be a success due to the inspiration his mother and sister had given him led him to also sacrifice. He grew reserved and guarded. The more successful he got, the less friends he had. Not necessarily because they changed, but because he had, and he wasn't sure if they had been there for him or for his success.

When he was drafted, he worked that much harder. His girlfriend broke up with him – something he couldn't blame her for – and it freed up even more time to focus. He played one season in the minors before being brought up to the Gulls in order to back up their starter, Misko Jarvinnen. He was an NHL player by the time he was nineteen and took on the starting role when Jarvinnen retired. His entire career was here, with the Gulls, which wasn't very common with goalies.

But once again, Ken had faith in his abilities and Brandon became unstoppable.

He knew he wasn't the friendliest guy. When the Gulls did fan events, he was called in and given an extra talking to be the event coordinator in order to ensure he would actually go out of his way to socialize with the guests. He was captain, after all, and that role came with more responsibility than most.

It was ironic, actually, when Ken suggested him as captain in the first place.

"You're the hardest working player on this team," Ken had pointed out. It had changed his life; Brandon had Ken's words memorized. "I don't give a shit if you can't talk. You can play. You can inspire. You can lead. That's what a captain must do. He must stand tall and hold it together when his team is falling apart. You do that every night."

With Ken's recommendation, Brandon was awarded the C his third season, with a unanimous vote by his team.

He earned that C, and he continued to earn it. He knew one of the things he had to work on was his interactions with people so he decided to do something about that during the summers and force himself to date. Nothing ever stuck but at least he could practice opening up to people, putting himself on the line whether he was asking a beautiful woman out or breaking up with her. He never let things get serious because he had never met anyone who had captured his full interest and he stayed celibate during the season in order to focus solely on the game.

But he liked dating, he found, and once the season was over, he looked forward to meeting new people he knew wouldn't last more than a few months in his life.

Until Seraphina.

At first, she was just another pretty girl he had seen in passing. He knew she was one of Ken's granddaughters but she was in school and didn't really involve herself in hockey-related events. Then, Ken was murdered, he wanted more money, and Seraphina inherited the team. This girl with no experience. He thought for sure they were going to let him go, if not because of his asking price, then definitely because he was a suspect.

But she didn't.

And that was when he knew she was different.

When Katella got that call in the nightclub – he couldn't even remember the name due to the fact that he wasn't paying any attention and didn't actually care to be there – his entire body tensed. He knew something had happened. He knew Seraphina was in trouble.

"Is everything okay?" Brandon asked her, shouting over the loud music after Katella put away her phone.

Katella looked up at him with her green-gold eyes and instantly, he could read her like a book. She wasn't as closed-off like her younger sister was, and, in this moment, he was grateful for that. No, everything was *not* okay. Something clearly happened to Seraphina, and whatever it was, it wasn't good.

Brandon clenched his teeth together and reached out one hand, gently placing it on her shoulder and giving it a squeeze. "Please, Kat," he said in a tight voice. He hated saying please at all, but he knew this was important. He didn't care about putting his pride aside if it got him information of Seraphina's well-being. "Tell me what happened."

"She's okay," she assured him, and Brandon could see he was telling the truth. "But she's coming back now. He tried something..."

"What?" Brandon snapped. He hadn't meant to but he couldn't stop it if he tried. He clenched his jaw and tried to control himself. Seraphina needed him to be calm when she came back.

And he would be. For her.

Chapter 7

WHEN SERAPHINA MADE it back to the hotel, Katella was
waiting in the lobby for her. She looked frustrated, pacing with
her arms crossed over her chest, her heels clacking on the tile
floors. When she caught sight of Seraphina, she immediately
went over to her sister and wrapped her up in a warm hug.

"Sera, are you okay?" Katella asked, pulling back and
looking at her sister with serious green-gold eyes.

Seraphina nodded. "He felt my thigh," Seraphina told her.
"You know, that scene in Legally Blonde? That's basically what
happened. It's not-"

"Do not say it's not a big deal," Katella snapped. Her face
softened. "Sorry. I'm just really pissed right now." She inhaled
deeply, like she was trying to calm herself down. "Negan is at
the club still, waiting for me to text."

"No, I'm not."

At that moment, Negan appeared, coming to stand beside
Katella. He looked good in a black collared shirt and dark jeans.
His dark hair was somewhat messy and his dark eyes were
narrowed and serious. His eyes took in Seraphina, making sure

that she wasn't injured and that she was all right. When he was satisfied with what he saw, he turned back to Katella.

"Everything okay here?" he asked.

Katella didn't respond. Instead, she kept her eyes focused on Seraphina and perked her brow, indicating that they were waiting on her response.

"I'm okay," Seraphina said.

"I know you're okay but maybe we should file some kind of police report," Katella said. "Just to document that this happened."

"Kat, this is Vegas," Seraphina said. "Do you know how many crimes happen in one night here? Do you really think they're going to take a police report because one of the wealthiest men here felt me up? So many other women get felt up-"

"He what?" a familiar voice snapped. Seraphina felt her face turn red as she peeked over her shoulder and found Brandon Thorpe standing beside her, a pinched look on his face that resembled nothing short of fury.

"It was no-"

"He felt her up," Katella interrupted, shooting her sister a look that said, *Don't downplay this; this is serious.* "Apparently, they were having an argument in the car as they were driving to the restaurant and he felt her up to prove his point so she punched him in the face. That's when she called."

"We should probably go somewhere private," Brandon said, glancing around. A couple of people stopped to stare at Brandon and Negan, having recognized the hockey players.

"Let's go to the suite," Katella suggested before Seraphina could interject and say she was okay. Seraphina shot her sister a look and Katella gave her one back that seemed to say, *Stop. You'll thank me later.*

So she bit her bottom lip to keep her mouth shut and allowed Katella to lead the foursome up to their suite.

"Harper and Emma are still downstairs with the rest of the team," Katella murmured as they stepped inside sleek elevators.

"I told them I would text them when you got here to let them know you were okay but I didn't think it was necessary to have them leave when they really don't get to hang out with their boyfriends in Vegas during the season."

Seraphina nodded in agreement. She already felt bad that Negan and Brandon weren't enjoying their night. She didn't want to be the reason people were leaving a good time.

"Do you want to talk about it?" Katella asked.

"I can go," Negan said in his gruff voice. Seraphina wasn't sure if he was being polite or if he was just uncomfortable to be there in the first place. She didn't want him to stay if he didn't want to.

"It's up to you," Seraphina told him as they walked in front of the suite.

"Why don't you go get some ice," Katella said, popping open the door with her keycard. They walked inside and Katella handed Negan the bucket. "We need to ice her hand."

He nodded and Katella led Seraphina to her bed in the master suite.

"Sera," she said. "I'm going to make sure Negan knows where he's going."

"I'll stay with her," Brandon offered quickly, stepping into the room.

Katella gave her a sister a look, asking if she was okay with being here by herself with Brandon. Her face was stoic, all teasing and playfulness gone. Seraphina gave her sister a curt nod and Katella disappeared out the door, leaving her and Brandon alone.

The room suddenly felt heavy but not uncomfortably so. If anything, it felt like there was a lot of unspeakable things between them, things that were bursting at the seams to be said.

"Are you all right?" Brandon finally asked.

Seraphina picked her head up and gave him a curious look. His face was pinched, his brow furrowed. He seemed to be debating to say something but something was holding him back.

"My hand hurts," she finally said, looking down at her right hand. It was red and swollen but numb so the pain was masked, at least for now. "I punched him twice."

"Twice?" A ghost of a smile danced across his lips.

Seraphina shook her head and looked away.

"So what happened?" he asked. She could sense the eagerness in his tone was tightly controlled so it came out odd and firm.

"You were right about him, Brandon," she told him, leaving her fingers together.

"I didn't want to be right about him, Sera," he told her slowly. He took a step towards her, hesitated, but pushed himself to the edge of the bed and took a tentative seat next to her. "I wanted this to work out the way you wanted it to work out."

"He was just saying really dumb, offensive things," she told him, her eyes on her lap. "And I just told him he was saying dumb, offensive things. And he slid his hand up my thigh and I punched him. And when he called me a dramatic bitch and said something about how I couldn't control myself with you, I punched him again."

Brandon clenched his jaw and looked away, rolling his fingers into fists.

"I should have-"

"There was nothing you could have done." She placed her hand over his in the same way he had done for her on the airplane. She didn't expect that it would make everything right again, she highly doubted she would be able to calm him down, but she could show him without words that she was here for him for as long as he needed her. She wouldn't run away from his silence. "In fact, I should have listened to you in the first place. At the very least, I should have researched the guy, especially after you told me you had personal experience with him. I just…" Her eyes dropped to her lap. "It's important to me that the team gets the recognition it deserves. My grandfather broke his back working for this team, creating it and building it, and he still never got to see us get into the playoffs. Right now, we're a wildcard entry for the Pacific Division and that's awesome, as long as we keep the momentum going. I would love to actually get a seed in the Pacific, rather than a wild card spot, just to guarantee we'll get there."

"We have nothing to prove to anybody, Sera," he told her, his brows furrowed as he regarded her with a passionate look. It wasn't something she was used to seeing on his face and it made her take pause because she was captivated by it and wanted to memorize it because his eyes turned a shade of green she had never seen before.

He was utterly beautiful.

"Let our talent speak for itself," he continued. "You made some amazing acquisitions over the summer. Negan, Ryan, all those guys. You somehow managed to resign Dimitri Petrov even though he was going through his own family issues. And you managed to resign your jackass goalie who was trying to hold out for more money all of last season."

Seraphina chuckled and looked away. She didn't do well with compliments but they were facts, weren't they? There was no reason to feel discomfort at all.

"We're going to come together." He took her hands in his. "I promise you. Whether we're placed or in a wildcard, who cares? We're going to get to the wildcard this season. You're going to make Gulls' history. We all are. But it will be because of you." He brought her fingers to his lips, never taking his eyes off of her. "If you can have faith in me, even though people thought I killed your grandfather, you can have faith in a team you helped build. Not just Ken, but you, too."

Seraphina nodded. "I guess it's just hard for me to believe that I could affect the team, make positive changes," she said. "I'm trying to do what my grandfather did because I feel that was what he would have wanted. He would want me to keep things consistent. Do research. Don't rock the boat. Letting players go because of the Vegas draft, letting others go to free agency, picking players up that haven't been playing well… That all scared the shit out of me. But it's working and I want to make sure my grandfather's values aren't being forgotten just because he's gone."

Brandon was silent for a moment. He seemed to be taking everything in, letting her words sink in. Finally, he cocked his head to the side and tentatively said, "I think, sometimes, you put too much pressure on yourself to be your grandfather and to live a life you think he would want when you should be focused on living a life *you* want."

Seraphina furrowed her brows. "What do you mean?" she asked.

"Your grandfather raised you and your sister and you both had special connections with him," he said. "I think you clung to the idea of making him proud and lived your life that way. A life he would approve of, not necessarily a life you actually want. Look at Katella; when your grandfather was alive, she got involved with his best center at that time. Do you think he would have approved of that?"

Seraphina pressed her lips together, remembering her grandfather's reaction when Katella told him what happened. "He wasn't happy," she said.

"But did Katella break things off with Peters even though he wasn't happy?" Brandon asked.

Seraphina shook her head. "No," she said. "She basically told my grandfather that she was going to be with Matt whether he liked it or not. He could either get on board and support her or he could not support it and there would be tension between them. But no matter what, they were going to be together."

"And what happened?" Brandon asked. "Ken accepted it."

"Yeah, but Kat isn't-"

"I don't care if she doesn't have your job title, Sera," he said. "Maybe things are slightly different for you both but you think that focusing solely on the team is going to make your grandfather happy when the truth of the matter is he would want you to be happy period. Your job in life is not to please him but to please yourself."

He picked up her chin with the tips of his fingers and looked her in the eyes. "Come on, Sera," he murmured slowly. "You know he wouldn't want you putting so much effort into his memory than you would your own life."

Seraphina clenched her teeth together. She wanted to tell him he didn't know her grandfather the way she did but that wasn't exactly true. Because what Brandon said made sense and it sounded like something her grandfather would tell her. She just hated when people talked about her grandfather like they knew him as a way to give her advice.

The truth of the matter was, no one knew him the way she and Katella did. But Brandon also had a good connection with him. She couldn't take that away either.

Chapter 8

SERAPHINA SWALLOWED, her eyes wide. She nodded her head and then realized she was answering a question he hadn't asked. She felt her cheeks turn red but she tilted her head up to lock eyes with him, letting him know that she wanted that as well. Very, very much.

When he met his lips with hers, she felt her entire body light up, her chest and pelvis and fingertips bursting with light and weightlessness. She felt whole, complete, the entire world suddenly right. And Seraphina was glad that this happened, that she boarded that plane even though she begged Katella to drive, she was glad she went to this stupid meeting and got into a fight with Brandon about it and bought the dress and had Katella do her hair and makeup. And she was glad she pushed Brandon in the lobby because then he kissed her the first time and this was just as sweet as the first time and her entire body tingled and she felt special and beautiful and everything wrong that had happened was suddenly right again.

She didn't even regret Phil Bambridge and what happened between them. She didn't regret hurting her hand and kissing Brandon in public, in front of Bambridge and -

It was all worth it. All of it. It was all worth it because it led to this moment and she wouldn't trade this moment for the world.

He slowly slid his tongue across her bottom lip and she opened her mouth slightly. She didn't even hesitate because she wanted the kiss to get deeper. She wanted to have this moment go on forever. She didn't want it to stop. And as long as he wanted to kiss her, she wouldn't push him away. Not now. He took full advantage of the fact that she opened up for him and tilted her head back even further so he could become acquainted with every crevice of her mouth. It was almost as though he was worried this would be the only time he ever kissed her and he wanted to prolong it as best as he could so he could memorize it to the best of his abilities.

His fingers were tangled in her hair, gently tugging at her roots so she felt pressure in her scalp. It wasn't painful; if anything she felt her thighs moisten at the tug, at the kiss, and his scent. He smelled clean and masculine, like the ocean at night. She reached up with her left hand - she couldn't clutch anything with her right hand since it hurt now. And more than anything else, at least she was here with him in this moment.

When they had to break for air, Brandon pressed his forehead against hers, just closing his eyes and taking a deep breath.

"I've wanted to do that for a very, very long time," he said in a raspy voice.

"I'm glad you did," she replied back.

"I hated watching you walk away," he told her before placing a kiss on her neck. She shivered and clutched him closer to her. She tilted her head to the side so he had access to her throat. "When Katella said something happened, I..." He let his voice trail off and he placed a kiss on her pulse before pulling back just slightly so he could lock eyes with her. "I didn't know what happened so I didn't know what to feel. It was a bunch of feelings all at one time. I was livid. I was furious. I was worried." He clenched his jaw together so tightly it popped and he cradled her cheek in his hand. The look on his face was fierce but his touch was gentle. The confliction of the two made Seraphina shudder and she couldn't help but lean into his touch. He had never talked this much about his feelings before. She wouldn't dare interrupt him. "Katella didn't tell me anything, not at first. And I understand, I guess. Who am I, anyway? But when you called again and she left, I made Negan tell me. And then I followed him to you. Because I had to make sure you were okay. I had to see for myself that you were okay."

"I didn't realize how worried you were about me," she murmured, though her cheeks were warmed with happiness.

"Of course I was worried about you," Brandon said as though it was the most obvious thing in the world. In fact, he almost seemed offended that she hadn't realized it in the first place. "Sera, I don't think you realize…" He let out a little growl and looked away.

"If I don't realize something," Seraphina said slowly, carefully, "it's because I was never told anything."

"I shouldn't have to tell you for you to know how I feel about you," he told her.

"Of course you do," Seraphina said. "I'm not a mind reader, Brandon. And you're so closed off from the rest of the world, if I did have to guess, I would assume you wanted nothing to do with me."

"That's bullshit," he said before clenching his teeth together.

"It's not, actually," Seraphina said. "When you came into my office yesterday, we talked more than we have since we first met each other. How am I supposed to know your feelings are different? You're supposed to tell me!"

"Or I could show you," Brandon said before he leaned forward and claimed her lips once again.

Seraphina's head with spinning with possibilities. She felt her nipples harden as his hands traced the curves of her body, letting his fingers trail against her breasts, against her hips. When he began to untie the dress, he kept his eyes on hers. She knew, in that moment, that he was in love with her. That it should have been clear from the get-go, and the fact that it wasn't didn't mean anything. It was there, deep inside of him. She could see it now.

The dress crumbled to the ground, leaving her in nothing but a sheer pair of lacy boy shorts and her jewelry. Seraphina watched as Brandon gulped, taking her in, his eyes respectfully feasting on the view she gave him. Her nipples were hard due to the cold, residual effects from the kisses they had just shared. Without taking her eyes off of him, she slowly began to remove her earrings, placing them on her nightstand as he went to close and lock her bedroom door.

This was going to happen. They were really going to make love.

She stepped out of her heels by the time Brandon returned, feeling more naked than she ever had in her entire life. She wasn't a virgin by any means – before Brandon, she had had two guys she had slept with while they had been in relationships – and while she had appreciated the sex for what it was, it didn't seem to be that big of a deal for her.

That would change, she knew, with Brandon.

He started pulling off his own clothes as he walked over to her so there was a trail of them leading over to where Seraphina waited by the bed. He placed both hands on her cheeks and kissed her, pressing his chest against hers. He started heading to the bed, Seraphina still wrapped in his arms, up until her knees hit the back of the bed. He gently pushed her back before he climbed on top of her. She could feel his hardness press into her hipbone and she moaned.

He trailed kisses down her throat, across her collarbone, between her breasts. His fingers slipped between the thin material of her and he hissed when his fingers slipped between her folds to find how slick she was. She let out a groan and he nearly ripped the flimsy material in two.

"Do you have anything?" she asked when she was completely naked underneath him.

He shook his head. "To be honest, I hadn't expected…" He let his voice trail off. "We can wait. I can go down to the lobby and-"

Seraphina cut him off with a kiss. "We have tonight," she told him as though it was the most obvious thing in the world. "I don't want to waste it."

He nodded once and kissed her long and hard. From there, he positioned himself on top of her and slowly entered her tight core. She groaned when he entered and every muscle inside of him tensed.

"Jesus Christ," he breathed out. "You are so goddamn tight, so goddamn wet. I can't move or I'm going to come inside of you right now."

Seraphina groaned. She pushed her brows together as she felt herself get wetter and wetter with every word he said. She bit the bottom of her lip as she got used to his size, the way he stretched her core like it was his, like she belonged to him and this was his right as owner of her core.

This felt right. And glorious. And Jesus Christ, her head was spinning. She couldn't even think straight.

He filled her up entirely, wrapping himself in her warmth. There was a little bit of pain, but the rush caused butterflies to dance in her stomach and her arms weaved around his shoulders and pulled him closer to her. She needed there to be no air between them, no space. She had waited too long for this moment and now that it was finally happening, she wanted to take her time and really feel it because she didn't know she they would get this chance again.

"You're so goddamn beautiful," he kept saying over and over again, his lips on her skin so when he spoke it vibrated against her surface. His lips were soft against her, gentle but passionate.

His voice, low and hungry and raw, gave her goosebumps and she couldn't suppress a groan as he continued to slowly rock

56

back and forth inside of her. It would seem he didn't want to rush, there was no need to rush, and he was focusing on speaking in order to keep his passion at bay. Every time he moved, he sent lightning to her core and her thighs spread to give him more access to her.

Her grip on him was tight. She didn't want him to leave her, didn't want him to ever separate himself from her body. It was stupidly romantic but if he pulled out, she felt that she would lose a piece of her, that she would feel somewhat empty when compared to him being inside of her, surrounding her.

He looked down at her with piercing green eyes. She looked back up at him, even though her first instinct was to look away. Eye contact during sex was ideal, certainly, but it also exposed her ever more than she already was. Sure, she was naked but look into her eyes meant seeing into her soul and she wasn't sure she was ready for anyone to do that. But she couldn't look away. It didn't matter that she wanted to, he wouldn't let her.

The look on his face was pure awe, like he couldn't quite believe this was happening and that it felt this right. Her eyes narrowed. He was just as vulnerable as she was. She had never expected to see him look this way, to look at her this was at all. She knew he cared for her but didn't realize how deep it went until now, until this moment.

Her pelvis started to tingle as he moved deeper inside if her at a consistent rate. His thrusts were deep and firm, not too fast, and she angled her hips so hit her just right...

It wasn't long before she felt the familiar tingle start to bubble up in her pelvis, like a shaken up soda can ready to be cracked open. What took her by surprise was the fact that she hadn't needed to stimulate herself in order to achieve orgasm but she wasn't going to question it. Her breathing got shallow, her forehead wrinkles, and just as she reached her peak, a smile eclipsed her face.

He knew, too. He kept his thrusting steady and she shattered around him. It was like sunshine melted around her and she was bathing in the afterglow.

Brandon kissed her cheeks her nose, her chin, her lips.

"Are you good?" he asked in a gentle voice. It was only then did Seraphina realize he had stopped moving. "Because we're not finished yet."

Chapter 9

SERAPHINA OPENED her eyes to a shadowed room, a heavy arm wrapped snugly around her waist. She felt her heart palpitations as last night flashed through her head and her entire body warmed the same way the sun would warm her body.

She and Brandon had had sex. She and Brandon had had sex and it was glorious and wonderful and it was literally the best thing she had done for herself in a long, long time. She stretched and refused to let herself think about what this meant and getting out of bed. Once she did that, the dream would be over and reality would hit and they would have to move on. Because they couldn't do this more than once.

Right?

If Brandon even wanted to.

"I can hear you thinking," he murmured.

She smiled and buried her face into his shoulder, trying to hide her blush. He tilted his head down and kissed the top of her head, rubbing her arm with his hands and giving her goosebumps.

"When is your morning skate?" she asked him, opening her eyes and tilting her head back so she could look at him.

His hair looked messy and adorable, his eyes bright but tired. He maintained a good grip on her waist. She liked to think it was because he didn't plan to let her go anytime soon, which was fine by her.

"Eight," he murmured. "So in an hour and a half. We're away so we skate earlier."

Seraphina nodded. She wasn't surprised that she woke up early. Unlike her sister, she preferred mornings and it was difficult for her to stay up past ten o'clock at night unless she had a very good reason to do so. And Brandon was a very good reason.

"I knew that," she said.

Her right hand was still swollen and it was hard for her to curl her fingers around anything solid but she could trail her fingers up and down his shoulder.

"You coming?" he asked.

"I did," she said with a grin. "Multiple times."

He chuckled and kissed her cheek. "Should we talk about it?" he asked, perking his brows.

Seraphina sighed through her nose. "Talking about it makes it real," she murmured. "Which means we would have to figure out where to go from here. Or it can be a beautiful, one-time thing."

Brandon furrowed his brows. "A one-time thing?" he said, cocking his head to the side. "I don't want it to be a one-time thing, Sera. I've been waiting for this moment since I first met you." He pressed his lips together and looked away, almost as though he hadn't meant to say that, but it had come out of his mouth anyway. "Anyway, I don't want this to be just once."

"Brandon," she murmured, looking at his collarbone. She had never thought something like a collarbone could be sexy. But she was starting to find little things on Brandon that were sexy, like the corded muscle in his forearms or the line in his thighs.

"Sera," he returned, his voice a little more forceful than hers. He wasn't being aggressive; rather, he was being direct. And he wanted her attention. Her eyes snapped into his and they were a fierce green color, like grass under the sunlight. "Please."

Her eyes widened. She knew Brandon well enough to know that he wasn't the type of guy to say please. He just didn't do that. This clearly meant a big deal to him and she felt guilt start to pool in her stomach at the fact that she wasn't taking this as seriously as she should have.

"I'm sorry, Brandon," she said. "I don't know what to tell you."

He seemed surprised by her response and immediately pulled away from her. The look he gave her made her entire heart break. Crack. She thought she had been hurt before. Even her grandfather's death, something she felt each and every day, hadn't weighed her down in this way. Because she could stop this. She could make him take her back in his arms and kiss her again and make love to her and make all of this just go away.

But she didn't take it back.

How could she?

"Tell me what you feel, Sera," he said. There was a tone to his words that was almost begging. But that was impossible because the last person Seraphina would think would ever beg was Brandon Thorpe. "Tell me what you want. Because I've been putting myself on the line here the past twenty-four hours and I feel like you aren't reciprocating. And it's hard for me to open up. So I'd like to hear how you feel now."

"Brandon, I-" She stopped herself. Why was this so difficult? All she had to do was put into words how she felt. Her eyes locked on his and she took a deep breath. "Brandon, I love you." Once the three words came out, more did, too. "I'm crazy about you. I can't stop thinking about you. You're all I dream about. And maybe that was too much information and you

think I'm some weird stalker now but I swear I'm not. I just...
Being with you is something I want more than anything."

Brandon pressed his lips together and crinkled his brow. He
was waiting for the other foot to drop, she realized, and she
hated the fact that what he was waiting for was going to happen.
That as much as she wanted him, she couldn't be with him. At
least, not right now.

"I've never felt this way about anyone else," she continued,
craning her head to look at him. She wanted him to understand
how serious she was being. They didn't know each other that
well, couldn't read each other's faces just yet, but if she
portrayed herself as open maybe he could discern how genuine
she was being now. "And I don't want to ruin your reputation,
either."

Brandon shot her a look. "How would you ruin my reputation if we were together?" he asked. "Come on, Seraphina.
Don't play dumb."

"If you're sleeping with me, people would assume you slept
your way to the top," Seraphina pointed out. "Everything
you've sacrificed, your mom' sacrificed, your sister sacrificed,
would mean absolutely nothing because it was known that you
and I are sleeping together. Nobody would believe you earned
any of your triumphs, unless you think earning them through
great sex counts. People won't take you seriously."

"Do you really think the guys on our team would think
that?" Brandon asked.

Seraphina shrugged. "I honestly don't know, Brandon," she
said. "But I need to protect you and I need to protect myself.
This is my grandfather's legacy and I will not have his name
tarnished because his granddaughters can't seem to keep their
legs closed around the players."

Brandon furrowed his brow. "Is that what you think this
was?" he asked. "You spreading your legs?"

"You're looking at this from a male perspective," Seraphina
pointed out. "The problem is, I, a woman with blonde hair and

big boobs who did absolutely nothing to earn this team in the first place, am not a man. I am a woman and as a woman, I am under way more scrutiny than my grandfather ever was. And you know what? That's partly deserved. I didn't go to business school and I didn't know much about hockey before suddenly being forced to. But other stuff is way more bullshit than you guys have to deal with." She pressed her lips together and looked away. "Ask your sister."

Brandon's eyes narrowed at the mention of his sister. "Excuse me?" he said.

"Ask your sister," she repeated. "I'm sure she'll have some idea of what I'm talking about."

"I'm sure my sister would pick my side-"

"This isn't about picking a side, Brandon," Seraphina said. "This is about what women have to deal with on a constant basis with positions of power in a male-dominated career. I'm not here to talk about feminism and equality even though those discussions should have their place at some point in the NHL but talk to your sister. Ask her what she went through playing hockey in Canada and everything she had to deal with. I guarantee you she has her own stories."

"What does my sister have to do with you and me?" Brandon asked. "I'm not saying you're wrong, but what does that have to do with us?"

"She doesn't have anything to do with us," Seraphina allowed. "But women have different expectations placed on them than men do. We're out under more of a microscope if we have positions of power, and if we don't, we're ignored completely. If you and I were to be whatever we were going to be, it would be complete hell. You would get ridiculed completely. All the hard work and dedication and sacrifice you put into this career, including everything your family did for you when you were a kid, would be for nothing. People wouldn't take you seriously. Your skill would come into question completely."

"You think I give any type of shit about that?" Brandon

asked through gritted teeth. His eyes sparked with anger and it broke Seraphina's heart to see him look at her this way. It made her feel entirely wretched, but she knew she was right. She was protecting him. "You think I care what people think of me? And how I got here? My skills speak for themselves. I have nothing to prove to anybody. And for you to think that I would care..." He clenched his jaw. "You don't know me at all."

"What do you expect?" Seraphina asked. "You don't tell me anything. You don't have conversations with me. A couple of days ago was the first time you talked to me about something not totally hockey related."

"You want to know how I feel, Sera?" he asked. "I'm crazy about you. I'm so fucking in love with you I don't know what to do with myself. I stay away because I don't want to be around you, I don't want you to realize it. Because I can't be around you and not want to touch you. I want to be with you. I want to be around you. And I know you feel the same way about me. I know you do."

"It doesn't matter what I feel," she told him but he interrupted her before she could say anything else.

"Of course it matters," he said. "Of course it does. If you feel the same way about me, there's no reason for us not to be together."

Seraphina crossed her arms over her chest and looked away. Her heart was heavy in her chest, sinking down to the pit of her stomach. "What do you want from me, Brandon?" she asked him softly. "What do you want me to do? I've already told you we can't be together. Maybe you can't see it, but I can. I know what is being together would do to you and-"

"Yeah," he said. "It would be the best thing that's ever happened to me. Even better than playing hockey. Being with you would surpass that." He clenched his jaw and looked away.

Seraphina's eyes teared up but she couldn't let him see how much this was breaking her. "You should go, Brandon," she told him, not able to look at him while she did so. "I'm not going to be able to tell you what it is you want to hear."

Brandon's mouth dropped open. She had never seen him look surprised before. But then he got a hold of senses, clenched his teeth together, and left. It was only then did Seraphina feel safe enough to release the tears she had been holding back.

Chapter 10

"WHAT THE FUCK, SERA?" Katella asked, throwing a piece of scrambled egg at her sister so it landed on her cheek. "Why did you do that? You went to bed with the love of your life – we all heard you and it wasn't exactly helpful when we're trying to get in the mood with our own guy, thank you very much. And then you let him go after a very tense conversation, no morning sex before the skate, and no food in his stomach? Are you insane? Why would you do this?"

Seraphina furrowed her brow, her eyes glassy. "I don't know," she said in a soft voice. She wasn't going to argue with Katella or explain her reasoning behind it. Not with how heavy her heart was in her chest. Not with how much pain her body was in.

Harper and Emma locked eyes with each other and Harper leaned forward, her forearms on the white table cloth. "Seraphina," she said in a gentle voice. "It's clear you have feelings for Brandon. You don't even deny it. He told you he has feelings for you. What's the big deal about seeing each other?"

"There's a conflict of interest," Seraphina said, picking her head up. "I don't need my other players saying I'm showing him

66

favoritism or I'm not putting him on the trading block because I want him here with me."

"Would the players even say that?" Emma asked, cocking her head to the side. "Negan and Kat are dating and no one has mentioned anything. Granted, not everyone knows about them and it's a little different since she's not the official owner, but still."

"It's different," Seraphina pointed out. "We all know it's different." Her head dropped to her hand while her other picked at her food. She had scrambled eggs with cheddar, fresh fruit, and breakfast potatoes. This was some of her favorite food and she couldn't bring herself to be hungry. Which was crazy because she was always hungry. It was part of her nature. Especially when it came to breakfast. "I'm the owner and manager. I have to set the example."

"Listen, Sera," Katella said, her tone no-nonsense with no room for arguing. "I'm not trying to be a bitch here but I have to in order for you to get this. Brandon Thorpe isn't the type of guy you meet often in your lifetime. He isn't going to wait around for you to realize he's worth taking a risk for and being with. If you can't show him this, if you can't be with him, he is not going to wait around for you. Do you understand this?"

Seraphina dropped her fork so it clattered to the plate and her hands found her face as tears spilled out of her. She started sobbing. Not cute sobbing where the girl was still pretty and onlookers felt compassion and sympathy. Seraphina was bawling, with excessive saliva spilling out of her mouth, snot running down her nose, her mascara from last night taking over her cheeks, her hair frizzing because her face was hot, red, and blotchy. The sounds she was making should not be coming out of a human and her shoulders jumped as each sob racked through her body in a jerky, twitchy motion.

She took ugly sobbing to a whole new level.

"Of course I know this," Seraphina replied, more saliva coming out of her mouth.

"This is the worst thing that's ever happened since Papa died and I don't... I don't know what I can do to fix it."

"It's a lot easier than you're making it out to be," Emma said gently, coming over to Seraphina and placing her hand on Seraphina's shoulder. "Seraphina, love is complicated, yes, and not everything is black and white." Seraphina tilted her head up and looked at her friend. Her face was sticky with drying streaks of tears on her face and she knew she probably looked absolutely ridiculous. "Your decision right now is not that complicated. You either want to be with him or you don't."

"And dragging it on and leading him on isn't going to help the situation," Harper pointed out. "I know some guys like the chase because they find it challenging but Brandon Thorpe seems like a pretty straight forward guy who wouldn't waste his time with stuff like that."

"I know," Seraphina muttered, looking down at her feet.

"Sera," Katella said. Her tone was hard to distinguish but her green-gold eyes were sharp and focused. There was an emotion there Seraphina had never seen before: disappointment. And it made Seraphina's gut clench with guilt. "I don't think you realize how much Brandon cares about you. When I got that first call from you, the one that told me what happened to you, he wouldn't let me out of his sight until he got some kind of answer of your well-being. He talked more to me then than he ever has. When I got the second call that told me you were here, he followed me like a goddamn shadow. When he first saw you, his eyes went everywhere on your body – up and down – making sure you weren't physically hurt. You realize it took everything in him to restrain himself from scooping you up in his arms, just to hold you because he was relieved what you endured with Bambridge wasn't worse?"

Seraphina felt quiet tears start to prick the corners of her eyes before slowly rolling down her cheeks. Her eyes were tired. They were sore and probably red. But she couldn't stop crying even if she tried. And right now, there was no reason to stop. Not when the tears were clamoring to get out of her body.

"I notice things like that, Sera," Katella continued. "Especially with someone as quiet and reserved and guarded as Thorpe. He was not closed-off or guarded. He was trying to be. He was holding himself back, yeah. But it wasn't working. *You* are the crack in his armor, Sera. You're his weakness." She pressed her lips together. "I think you're making a mistake. I'm always going to be there for you but don't complain about Brandon when he finds someone else who realizes that he's worth the risk and doesn't run away and hides from love. And that's what you're doing. You can dress it up any way you want but that's what you're doing and, quite frankly, it pisses me off."

"You think I want to taint Papa's legacy by dating one of his players as the owner and manager of the team?" Seraphina asked, wrinkling her brow and looking at her sister like she could not believe what she was insinuating.

"Papa is dead, Sera," Katella snapped. "Papa is dead and you have to be able to wrap your head around that. He isn't coming back. He isn't looking down on you with this anger and expectation to keep his values the same. If he had, don't you think he would have outlined something to tell you how to do your job? But he didn't, did he?" Katella slowly walked over to the closet, shaking her head. "Didn't he come to you constantly for opinions about whether or not he should trade someone or how he should handle a particular situation he was in? Do you think he would have done that if he was so concerned about doing everything right? Because you sure as shit didn't know anything about hockey then and he continued to go to you for advice."

Katella emerged from the closet in a bra and boy shorts and she began to slide on her outfit for the day - a white blouse and dark skinny jeans.

"Stop desecrating his memory by using him as an excuse to not be with Brandon," she finished.

"Excuse me?" Seraphina asked through gritted teeth, looking up from her plate to lock eyes with her sister. Harper was suddenly very interested in her phone and Emma excused herself quietly, disappearing into the restroom to shower.

"You heard me, Sera," Katella said, buttoning up her jeans. "Stop using Papa as an excuse for why you won't be with Brandon. You're making that choice because you're scared, not because of Papa, and to use him like that is just dishonorable."

"Dishonorable?" Seraphina asked. "Says the girl who can't keep her legs shut with his team."

"It isn't his hockey team anymore," Katella snapped, her eyes flashing emerald. "It's your hockey team. Yours. Papa is dead," she repeated. "Stop saying it's his team. It's yours."

Seraphina clenched her teeth together and curled her fingers into fists to keep her temper at bay. She knew what Katella was trying to do and she couldn't rebel against it - Ken was her grandfather too. If anyone got to claim ownership of him the way Seraphina had, it would be Katella. At the same time, it was difficult to understand how they both could have such different perceptions of the same man.

They both couldn't be wrong.

Katella pressed her lips together and kept from saying anything else. That was probably a good thing. Seraphina had said done pretty nasty things and she knew that eventually she would apologize for it but not now. Things were still heated between them and Seraphina was still reeling from what happened this morning with Brandon. She needed to get out of here, away from her friends, away from her sister. She threw on some workout clothes and headed to the hotel gym. She didn't even like working out but she needed a way to get all this excess energy out.

After a couple of hours in the gym, she glanced at the wall clock. Brandon would be leaving the morning skate right now. Her heart clenched in her chest and she forced everything down, she didn't want to feel this anymore.

At that moment, Katella walked in the gym in yoga pants and a tank top, her hair thrown up in a ponytail. Seraphina wasn't sure if she should hide or if she should let Katella find her because there was no way Katella was here to workout. As much as Seraphina didn't like working out, Katella liked it even less. She looked good in workout clothes but Katella preferred activity to straight-up exercise - she preferred hiking, soccer, and dance rather than walking on a treadmill.

When Katella found Seraphina on the treadmill, she nodded at her sister and started to head over. Seraphina tensed and froze. Any chance of avoiding Katella went out the window.

"Hey," she said.

Seraphina took out her earphones and nodded once. "Hey," she said, her voice tentative, still not sure how to respond. Still not sure what Katella wanted.

"I'm here to apologize," Katella said, her green eyes sincere. "I know I came out harsh and while I thought I was being helpful because I think it's important you realize that Brandon Thorpe -"

"I know, Kat," Seraphina said, placing her hands on her hips. "Trust me, I realize how amazing the guy is. With everything," she added, a small blush on her face.

"Good," Katella said with a nod. "I'm glad. But I still don't need to butt in and give you my opinion and make it seem like I'm telling you what to do. So I'm sorry for that." She reached out and cupped Seraphina's cheek with her hand, causing Seraphina to pick her eyes up and look at Katella. "I just want you happy, Sera. And I know Brandon would make you so happy. And if anyone deserves to be happy, it's you." She dropped her hand and took a step back. "Okay, that's all I wanted to tell you."

"Wait," Seraphina said. Katella stopped from turning around and raised a brow. "I'm sorry, too. I shouldn't have said what I said. That was completely underhanded of me and I'm sorry."

"You don't have to apologize," Katella said with a smile. Seraphina could tell that she appreciated the gesture, however. "You're my sister and ever since we were kids, you've been a brat. I'm the instigator, you're the brat." Seraphina laughed as Katella pulled her into a tight hug. "It's okay. I always forgive you."

Chapter 11

THE MORNING SKATE was not one of Brandon's best. He saved the majority of shots but not with the natural ease he was used to making saves with.

He couldn't get Seraphina out of his mind. He couldn't get the feel of her body from his hands, the taste of her out of his mouth, her scent out of his nose. He hated how stubborn she was being. He knew she had feelings for him, that she wanted to be with him just as badly as he wanted to be with her. And yes, he could understand her hesitation because whether he wanted to admit it or not, there was a conflict of interest.

But that didn't mean he had to like it.

And maybe he hadn't had to storm off and leave her in the morning without eating breakfast with her. And God, he wanted to kiss her just one more time, especially if they weren't going to be together. The look in her eyes broke his heart because he absolutely knew she loved him. He didn't doubt that for one second. It was actually adorable how awkward she got when she was around him.

That was what frustrated him more than anything.

Why sacrifice what they could be together?

But he knew. And he hated that it actually made sense. If she wasn't ready for a relationship or she didn't want to settle down, he could be annoyed, but she hadn't been with anyone in a long time. Until their night last night, of course.

He wouldn't let himself think about that, though. Her silky skin, the way her sky blue eyes turned dark when she took him in the first time, her perfect mouth. Everything about her got him hard and to know he would never touch her again was not something he wanted to even entertain at the moment.

He waited until he reached his hotel room before showering. A couple of the single guys were going to a pool party but he wasn't in the mood. Instead, he ordered a large thing of pasta just after eleven and ate the two thousand-plus calories the meal provided him. Then, he took a long nap before getting dressed and heading to the lobby to meet up with the team. The bus picked them up exactly at four thirty and delivered them to the nearby stadium just after four forty-five. From there, they assembled in the visitor's locker room where they warmed up by jogging around and playing hacky sack.

When it was six forty-five, they were dressed in their gear and ready for warmups. Brandon focused only on the sport. He had given himself time throughout the day to be frustrated by Seraphina's choice. Now, he had to be on point and couldn't afford any distractions.

The first period went by uneventfully. Brandon was on top of his game, his eyes sharp, his focus on point. His entire body was tense the whole period, except when there were scheduled commercial breaks. During those two minutes, Brandon liked to grab the water bottle sitting on top of his net, squirt the water in his mouth – since both goalies shared water bottles – and skate over to the bench. Not necessarily because Cherney called him over to talk or to talk with his goalie coach, but because it got him moving, relaxing his muscles and stretching them out. He always took care to look around for the ice girls who swept up the ice.

These girls were all beautiful but their makeup was overdone and their hair looked stilted and crunchy. They were wearing silver, sparkly mini dresses, which must have been cold for them but the smiles on their faces didn't reveal that they were cold if they were.

Brandon knew Seraphina, her sister, and a couple of the team's girls were sitting at glass seats rather than the suite Phil Bambridge had paid for. He didn't look at them outright, especially not Seraphina who looked beautiful in a simple red blazer, a white dress, and dark black flats, but he did notice them.

When he skated back to his net, the puck drop was to his left. This was his weak side – if he had a weak side – because while he caught left, he controlled his goalie stick with his right hand and he preferred to be angled in the right direction rather than the left.

The Blackjacks won the faceoff and immediately a skater positioned himself close to Thorpe in front of his crease. He wore 89 with the name Stevens on the back of his sweater.

Thorpe pushed Stevens out of his crease using his goalie stick at a horizontal angle. Technically, Brandon could have gotten called for crosschecking but unless it was an obvious hit, the referees usually let goalies get away with it.

"Heard about what happened last night," Stevens said, keeping his eye on the puck. Regardless, Thorpe knew his words were directed to him. "Your girl boss really gets around, doesn't she? First with you, then with my boss."

Brandon clenched his jaw but ignored him. He knew Stevens was trying to throw him off, trying to get into Brandon's head. It wouldn't work, even if they were insulting Seraphina.

"Maybe I can get on that, huh?" Stevens continued. "She's easy, right. You had her, Phil had her… She's drop dead gorgeous. What I wouldn't give to have those legs wrapped around me while I fucked her cunt with –"

And that was when Brandon couldn't control himself any longer. He dropped his gloves, threw off his mask, and went after Stevens with all he had. No one was allowed to talk about Seraphina that way. He didn't give a shit who it was or when it was, he wouldn't allow that to stand.

Brandon managed to get two good punches in right on Stevens's jaw. His hand hurt but it wasn't the kind of pain that exploded through his hand, cracked his bones and caused his blood to heat up. Or maybe it was and he just wasn't focused enough to notice. The noise was muted. He didn't see the crowd jump to their feet, clamoring to see a star goalie get in a fight with a third line nobody from a new team. Brandon was aware there was a chance he could injure his hand, which meant he'd be out for the rest of the season and, if they continued to play well and get points, playoffs. He had yet to make playoffs in his professional career and it was one of his goals he intended to achieve at some point. But now, he was willing to throw that away just to get the satisfaction of punching this asshole for running his mouth about the woman he loved, the woman who refused to be with him because of some messed up values that thought being with him would ruin both of them.

But the sound of his fist hitting Stevens's jaw, that loud pop, drowned out the rest of the noise. It was satisfying and the look on Stevens's face just added to the moment. He kept going as long as he could. Stevens, unfortunately, managed to get a couple of hits in. His face hurt but Brandon couldn't feel it. He had no idea how that made any sense but it was as though his mind registered the hit and he expected it to hurt, his adrenaline was coursing through his body quickly, he didn't even feel it. He would be bruised, definitely, but it didn't matter. His pain didn't matter just as long as he could inflict some of his own. Finally get this guy to shut the fuck up about Seraphina.

"You piece of shit," Stevens said, blood dripping out of his mouth like goddamn rubies. "You fucking like her, don't you? You stupid piece of shit. You really think she's going to be with you? That fucking slut will sleep with anyone to get her way. You know that right?"

Brandon kept his mouth shut. However, his fingers tightened and he managed to hit Stevens twice more before the refs forced him off of the skater. Even pulling him apart, Brandon tried to reach for him, tried to get at least one more punch in, but a linesman skated over and helped the referee keep them separated.

Stevens was laughing which only enraged Brandon even further but he let them push him off the ice and onto his bench. He didn't look at his team or the coaches as he made his way into the locker room. The only person who followed him was the trainer, probably to ensure he'd be able to play the next game. It didn't feel like he had broken his hand. Then again, he didn't feel much of anything.

When he made it to the locker room, he sat down on the bench in front of his locker and slowly pulled off his helmet. This wasn't like him. He didn't lose control. Even when he played triple A hockey back when he was a teenager and they talked about his sister and the father that left him when he was five. He stayed focused and won the championship. He didn't even flinch. And they said a lot of terrible things about his sister, pretty much in the same vein that they had about Seraphina.

And this was his sister.

Why had he allowed Stevens to get to him in the first place was beyond his comprehension. It might have to do with the fact that he was already an emotional wreck after what happened between him and Seraphina. He had finally confessed his feelings and she had told him she felt the same way. She said the words he had wanted to hear. They had been together. He got to feel what it was like to be inside of her and it surpassed everything he had imagined it would be. And then she took that all away this morning when she told him she couldn't - wouldn't - be with him.

He felt a variety of conflicting emotions pass through his body - anger, frustration, sorrow, loss. It was like everything he had hoped for was suddenly ripped from his hands, not for a good reason but because she was scared. Because that was the truth of the whole thing - Seraphina was scared. And instead of taking the risk and just testing the waters out with him, she had dismissed the idea. She wouldn't even let him talk about it, wouldn't even let him give his side.

"Looks like you didn't sprain or break anything," the trainer said. Brandon hadn't even realized he had been sitting next to him, looking at his hand. Was he so focused on his thoughts or was his hand so numb? "You'll be able to play not next game but the one after that."

Brandon nodded. "Did I get a misconduct?" he asked.

"Game misconduct," the trainer replied with a grin. "You beat the shit out of him."

Brandon smirked but didn't say anything in return. His intention wasn't to beat the shit out of him. It was to shut him up. It was to make him realize he couldn't talk about Seraphina that way, at least not to him.

"What happened?"

Brandon felt his guard go up. He didn't particularly like talking to people, not because he was a snob but because he didn't like to talk. Typically, he might have just shrugged and made a noncommittal sound but he wanted to try and be better.

"The guy was running his mouth and wouldn't shut up," Brandon told him.

The trainer chuckled. "He got what was coming to him then," he said.

Brandon nodded his head. He didn't say anything as the trainer walked back to the bench but his lips curled into a smirk.

Chapter 12

SERAPHINA HAD TO BLINK ONCE, twice, before she realized just what the hell had happened. She had seen Stevens chirp off to Brandon from the glass seats she purchased for her and her three girlfriends in lieu of joining Phil Bambridge in his private suite. This way, she was up close and personal with the action and could watch her team on the ice. She actually loved watching the game close up and considered investing in glass seats rather than a suite for next season.

With the change, she was able to see a lot more than she could from her suite. It was how she was able to see Stevens say something to Brandon as he positioned himself on the crease of the net as his team tried to cycle the puck behind Brandon's net and shoot it. At first, Brandon didn't respond to it. However, when the Gulls cleared it from their zone, with Zachary Ryan, Kyle Underwood, and Alec Schumacher racing up the ice to the other side, Stevens stayed put and continued to talk.

That was when Brandon said something back. Stevens smirked — it was easy to tell since he didn't wear a glass shield that protected his eyes from pucks or high sticks — and said something else. From there, Brandon dropped his gloves, ripped off his mask, and went after Stevens without hesitating.

Brandon got in a couple of punches, startling Stevens. It seemed like the right winger hadn't expected Brandon to actually to hit him. In fact, the crowd got silent for less than a second. Seraphina could hear a pin drop in the high seats before the entire stadium erupted. Almost everyone leaped from their seats. Seraphina only did because she wanted to see what was going on and she couldn't do that from the angle from her seat. Katella and Harper jumped up to encourage the fighting. Emma jumped up, her eyes wide, but she wasn't as vocal as the other two.

Stevens managed to a hold of himself and knock a couple of shots in. Seraphina winced but couldn't look away. For some reason, the refs were letting them go at it, probably to generate interest in the new hockey team. Which was nice, save for the fact that Brandon and even Stevens could get seriously injured. Not necessarily from the fight, but if they damaged their hands, that could very well bench them for a long time.

Because they were on skates, their reach gave them an advantage. Seraphina was worried his gear and extra goalie padding would make it more difficult for Brandon to stay upright. However, it was actually Stevens that wound up on his back, not Brandon. Typically, at this point, the fight would end. It was almost like a gentleman's arrangement.

That went out the window when Brandon kept punching Stevens even though he was on the ice.

That was when the refs ripped the two apart. Brandon had to be held back by a linesman because he wanted to continue to fight Stevens.

"What the hell happened?" Emma asked, her brown eyes wide as the foursome watched the referees lead both Brandon and Stevens back to their respective benches so they could get to their locker rooms.

"Hell if I know," Seraphina muttered. "Should I-"

"Yes," Katella said, turning her head to look at her sister. "No one can check on him except the trainers, and judging by how pissed he is, I highly doubt the trainers are going to be with him for very long. The same thing happened with Negan one time. He just lost it on someone so I went back to check on him. Maybe it wasn't my place but I've never seen him that pissed after a fight. Usually, he's amused, like he ran his big mouth and instigated the fight on purpose."

Seraphina pressed her lips together and nodded her head, slipping out of her chair and heading up the steep stairs in order to get to the locker. She wasn't entirely familiar with the layout of the rink, having turned down Phil Bambridge's offer to tour it earlier this morning, but thanks to a couple of helpful employees who worked in the food stand, she was able to make her way down to the locker rooms.

Besides Thorpe, there was one trainer there, icing his hand. When he noticed Seraphina, he straightened up.

"Nothing's broken, ma'am," the trainer, Jeff, told her. "He just needs to ice his hand and rest it. We might consider playing Jimmy in against Houston, but Thorpe should be all good to go in Phoenix a few nights from now."

Seraphina pressed her lips together and nodded. "Thank you, Jeff," she said. "I take it you have to get back to the game?"

He nodded his head. "I just came back to check on him. There are still a good ten minutes left to the game," he said. "I need to be on the bench. Just in case."

"Okay," she said with a nod. "I need to talk to Thorpe anyway."

When the trainer left, she turned her attention to Thorpe. He had his jersey and helmet off, and he was nearly completely void of the padding on his body. His skates were off to the side. He looked nothing short of furious. His green eyes were sharp and narrowed on the floor in front of him, his left hand was curled into a fist while the right one – his injured hand – was tense, at his side with ice covering it. He was sweaty, with his brown hair every which way.

He was a goddamn vision.

"Are you okay?" she asked him.

He didn't respond. Instead, he shot her a look that seemed to say, *Do I look okay?*

"What happened?" she asked, deciding to try a different tactic.

"I lost control," he said without looking at her.

"Is that all you're going to tell me?" she asked, trying to keep her frustration at bay. This was the last place where she wanted him to hide himself from her.

"What would you like to know, Sera?" he asked, throwing his eyes at her. They were filled with rage, with frustration, that when they landed on her, she flinched.

"Do you want to know that Phil Bambridge told his entire goddamn team about what he did to you but decided to leave out the part where you stood up for yourself? Or would you like to know that Bambridge also told him about our kiss, making you out to be a complete and utter puck slut? Do you want to know how fucking furious I was when he started telling me that he was going to try the same things with you because Bambridge made you out to be so easy and I indirectly helped him when I kissed you so publicly last night? Do you want to hear that you were right, that I get it now why you're hesitant to be with me because if you're with me, I'd never hear the end of it and people might think they can touch you and taste you and even look at you like you're theirs, like they have any chance to be with you? I could tell you about how fucking good it felt to punch Stevens over and over and I would have kept going if the refs hadn't pulled me off. That it was worth it, getting kicked out of the game."

Seraphina let out a shaky breath. "I didn't know," she murmured.

Brandon took a breath and glanced up at her. "Why would you?" he asked.

She took a seat next to him, keeping a respectful distance in case he didn't want her to touch him at all. "Can I do anything?" she said. She glanced at her hands in her lap. "You didn't have to defend me, Brandon."

He gave her a cutting look. "Of course I did," he told her as though it was the most obvious thing in the world. "He's not allowed to talk about you that way to me at all. I don't care what's going on between us. You're still my friend, Sera. You're still part of this team. You're still the one..." He let his voice trail off and Seraphina couldn't tell if there was more to the sentence than he let on.

"You also got kicked out of the game," she pointed out. She wanted to be angry at him for his selfishness but she couldn't find it in her to do so. Instead, she felt tired. Achey. Upset that she couldn't reach out and pull him into a tight hug. "I don't remember the last time a goalie got a game misconduct for fighting." She gave him a sideways grin. "It was kind of hot, to tell you the truth."

Brandon's lips curled up. "Really?" he asked, turning his torso towards her body and leaning close to her.

"Oh, yeah," she said, lifting her head up. "I've never had anyone fight for my honor before."

Seraphina tilted her head to the side so she could capture Brandon's eyes. For a moment, they just stared at each other. There was a comfortable silence that surrounded them, cloaking them in comfort. Brandon leaned forward and Seraphina didn't pull away. She watched as he softly placed his lips on hers and she sighed. This was what it was all about. This kiss made everything right and good and how could she have rejected this in the first place? It made absolutely no sense to her and she immediately regretted her decision to tell him she couldn't be with him because she could and she would and she was tired of running.

Without breaking contact with his lips, she climbed on top

of his lap and grinded against him. His hands immediately went to the small of her back, pressing against it as a way to keep her from changing her mind and getting off. She felt him respond immediately and her thighs erupted into goosebumps. Katella had judged her for wearing a simple dress to a hockey game but now she could use the fact that she had no pants on to her advantage.

She pulled her lips away from his do she could tilt her head to the side and whisper in his ear, "Take me."

Brandon pulled back so he could read her eyes. She wasn't sure what he saw but he didn't have to ask to confirm that that was what she wanted. She quickly reached underneath her skirt and moved over her underwear so he would be able to slip into her. He grabbed a towel and placed it underneath him before he pulled his pants down so his cock could spring free. Without hesitating, she climbed on top of him and he gripped her hips as she slid on top of him. She moaned and he let out a sigh, like he had been waiting for this moment for a while. He probably had been.

God, she was such a moron.

"I'm sorry," she told him as she waited before moving, as she waited to get used to him. "God, I'm so sorry."

"Shut up," he breathed out. "I forgive you. I forgive it all."

She started moving slowly, up and down his cock as she coated him in her juices. He let out a groan as his grip on her tightened. He started thrusting faster and she leaned back, giving her better access to her clit. She began to rub it as he helped her ride him. Her breathing came out in short, quick gasps.

It only took a moment but she felt her pelvis start to tingle with restrained build up. She was going to come soon and he knew it. His lips found her throat and she could feel him sucking on her skin. She was absolutely certain he was going to leave a mark on her and she didn't care. Not in this moment.

And when she shattered, she saw stars, and he came with her, like they were made from the same clay, carved as two halves when joined turned into one. And they were, she realized, they were.

Chapter 13

SERAPHINA RIGHTED her clothes and managed to get dressed and leave the locker room before the period ended, narrowly avoiding possibly a lot of questions from her players. She couldn't be too concerned with Brandon fixing himself back up. Not that he was going to go back on the ice at all. He received a game misconduct and now Jimmy Stafford was in net. She didn't think he was going to be suspended, thank God, and she hoped her rookie goaltender would be able to keep the Blackjacks at bay and come up with a win. The Blackjacks were chippy and had a lot to prove, but so did the Gulls. They needed the two points if she wanted to seed in the Pacific Division.

When she returned to her seat, Katella took one look at her and snorted. "Locker sex, Seraphina?" she asked. "Really?"

Seraphina felt her cheeks turn red. "I don't know what you're talking about," she muttered under her breath as the referees skated onto the ice.

The rest of the game went by in a blur. She actually felt pretty bad about not paying as much attention to it as she wanted to because she couldn't stop thinking about Brandon, about what they did, about what this all meant. She couldn't just tell him no now. She couldn't tell him they couldn't be together when it was all she wanted. He had told her him and Stevens had gotten into it because Phil Bambridge couldn't keep his mouth shut and his players had believed what he said instead of taken it with a grain of salt.

Which was fine. Understandable, even.

But to say Brandon was pissed was an understatement. He fucked her like he was still angry. Not with her but with what had happened to her. With what he couldn't stop. He had taken his anger out on Stevens when it really should have been directed at Bambridge. Of course, Stevens shouldn't have been running his mouth as a way to distract the goalie, especially since Stevens had no idea what had transpired between him and Seraphina the previous evening.

Brandon, luckily, didn't do any permanent damage to his hand. A long icing and tentative care, plus forty-eight hours of non-use would mean it would heal just fine. There was a slight chance Brandon could be suspended due to his aggression, but Seraphina doubted it since she had seen plenty of fights that were similar and none of the skaters got suspensions before.

"So?" Harper asked, furrowing her brow and giving Seraphina a look. "What happened?"

Seraphina felt herself blush and couldn't look Harper – or anyone else, for that matter – in the eye. "I guess Stevens began running his mouth to Brandon because Phil Bambridge can't keep his big mouth shut," Seraphina said, clenching her teeth together. "His entire team knows about me and Brandon, apparently."

"How the hell could they possibly know that?" Katella asked. "It wasn't as though they were in your room while you guys had sex last night."

"Oh." Seraphina realized she had forgotten to mention that she and Brandon had kissed before, in the lobby. "Brandon and I were arguing before Phil Bambridge even showed up to pick me up. He was trying to talk me out of going again and we ended up kissing. Phil Bambridge saw the kissing but he made no mention of it except when he tried to feel me up."

"Bambridge is probably pissed because you rejected him in favor of Thorpe," Emma said. "And running his mouth is his way of getting back at you."

Seraphina shrugged. "I can't begin to tease out his logic," she replied.

"But that doesn't explain why Brandon lost it," Katella pointed out. "So what if Bambridge told the whole team about you? How does that piss off Thorpe?"

Seraphina shrugged. "He wouldn't go into specifics," she told him. "All I know was that he continued to run his mouth and Brandon lost it. We're probably sitting him next game so his hand can recover." Before they could ask, she quickly added, "It's not broken or sprained, just sore, thank God."

Katella was quiet for an uncharacteristic amount of time. By now, she would have been in the middle of a long lecture about how good this was for everyone involved, what this meant, and what Seraphina should do.

"So what does that make you guys?" she finally asked, picking her eyes up to look at Seraphina.

"What does that mean?" Seraphina asked.

"It means," Katella said slowly, "are you and Brandon a thing now? I mean, clearly you just had sex in the locker room. And I'm not pointing that out to put you on the spot. More like, you guys can't sleep together and not be together."

"Why would you assume we were doing that in the first place?" There was an edge to Seraphina's voice she couldn't seem to control. She didn't particularly like what Katella was insinuating with her line of questioning. "You know I'm not that type of person, Kat."

"Honestly, after what happened between you and Brandon the past forty-eight hours, I really don't know who you are," Katella said. "At least when it comes to him. It's obvious he loves you, you reject him. He gets into a fight on the ice because some jackass is trash talking you and you have sex with him in the locker room."

Seraphina clenched her jaw. "It's complicated," she said with a shrug. "We haven't actually talked about what we are."

"Would you, though?" Katella took a long sip of her drink, her eyes on the glass even though it was clear she was talking to Seraphina. Harper was munching on a jalapeño pretzel while Emma was chowing down on some popcorn.

"Would I what?" Seraphina asked. She had bought a Kit Kat Bar because she had been craving chocolate but now she was in no mood to eat. Not even something sweet, which was odd since that wasn't typically like her. She could eat chocolate all the time if she had to.

"When you guys talk," Katella said, "and he told you he wanted you to be with him, would you be with him?"

Seraphina shrugged her shoulders. "I have no idea," she said, shaking her head. "We couldn't go public right away. We might not be able to go public at all, not even to the team. I wouldn't be surprised if someone tried to blackmail me for a spot on the team or someone tried to goad Brandon in another fight." She shook her head. "It wouldn't be a good idea."

"So you're saying you would keep it a secret?" Harper said, looking up from her pretzel and raising a brow.

"What other choice would I have?" Seraphina asked.

"I just think that the fact that Seraphina is even considering being with him, even if it is under the radar, is an excellent idea," Katella said. "Oh, look! Now Negan's getting chirpy with Stevens. I wonder if that jackass won't keep his mouth shut."

"Considering Bambridge told him everything that happened to me, it wouldn't surprise me if he was trying to get other players off the ice," Seraphina said and then shook her head. "I need to have a talk with the team after this. We're so close to a seeded spot that we can't risk it based on defending honor. They have to just deal with it."

"Oh, come on, Sera," Katella said with a fake pout. "It's so hot when they fight for our honor."

"True," Seraphina said, "but it's also stupid. Stevens is a third line nobody. It's his job to get star players like Zachary Ryan, Kyle Underwood, and James Negan off the ice for five minutes. The fact that he got Brandon Thorpe kicked out of the game is a fucking miracle."

"You better hope they don't realize he has feelings for you," Emma said, leaning forward and clutching her popcorn to her chest. "They could target you in order to get him off the ice."

"I think that was a one-time thing," Seraphina said. "I highly doubt he's going to lose control again the way he did with Stevens. He's not the sort of guy who gets into fights. I mean, he's a goalie."

"True," Harper said, nodding her head. "But you'd be surprised. Our guys fight a lot for skilled players. We have fourth-liners that would defend them, sure, but they defend themselves and the easy target is the significant other."

The game ended with a couple more tiffs on the ice between Negan and Stevens. Katella, of course, was on her feet and cheering for him. Her eyes were dark green and there was a particular smile that slithered onto her face. There was love and affection there, Seraphina noticed, but also lust and desire. Seraphina hid her own smile. She understood now why Katella loved the fighting in hockey. Before she knew The Code, knew that fighting was actually a strategy for the sport, she thought the entire thing was pointless.

But once she inherited the team, she realized fighting was a necessity. The team used it as a way to send a message that they weren't going to tolerate any roughing of their skilled players, the team used it as a way to regulate the game when the refs weren't calling anything, they used it as a strategy to get a skilled player off the ice, to get the fans into the game, and to inspire his team after they'd been scored on. And, after she watched Brandon engage in it as a way to defend her, she realized it was a draw for the females. Sure, some believed fighting took away from the sport and made it seem ridiculous rather than athletic but Seraphina had her mind changed and she was so glad she did.

Seraphina stepped into the locker room before the media and the team, who had just wrapped up a speech given by Cherney, parted ways to make room for her. She took a step on the bench so she could be seen. Her face was beaming with pride. Also, she had some awesome sex where she was standing but nobody else needed to know that.

"Guys," she began, "thank you so much for your hard work and dedication. Shoutout to Jimmy who stepped up when Thorpe decided to get himself kicked out of the game for losing his shit for some reason. I really wanted to win this one for personal reasons and I'm so glad you guys came through. We already have a wild card seed for the playoffs. Nothing is guaranteed obviously but if we play like we did tonight, we could make playoffs, boys!"

Everyone cheered and whistled.

"Alcohol on the plane on me!" she exclaimed.

More cheering.

"All right," she said. "Finish what you're doing here. Media will probably want to question you - even you, Thorpe. You better figure out a good reason why you completely lost it out there." She gave him a wink and he grinned back.

A look passed between them, a secret look that nobody else understood. A look that was just theirs.

Her heart skipped. This could work, she realized. This could work.

Chapter 14

WHEN THEY LEFT THAT EVENING, Seraphina was reminded that they had a mini-roadtrip before they flew back to Newport Beach. The Gulls were scheduled to play the Houston Rangers tomorrow and then the Phoenix Rattlesnakes two nights after that. She had completely forgotten that in all of her scheduling. When she realized if she traveled with the team, she would be expected to make an appearance at both games, Seraphina okayed it. She hadn't traveled with the team for her entire tenure and decided since she was already with them, it might be fun to watch them play as a visitor than just at home. She asked the girls if they wanted to go home because of some scheduled obligation but nobody took her up on her offer of flying them home. Even Emma, who always seemed to be busy, was able to go on the little getaway.

She sat with Brandon on the plane and the two held hands once again. It calmed Seraphina down just like it did before. Other than that, they did not touch. Seraphina still didn't know what this was, and just because she was open to seeing where it went didn't mean she needed to force her team into being around it.

Somehow, she fell asleep and her head hit Brandon's shoulder. She was out until the plane landed. Then, Brandon gently woke her up. She felt refreshed, safe. Glad she didn't have to worry about reacting to the plane landing. To her, that was always the worst part of being afraid to fly, that little bump that always occurred right after the plane touched the ground at that speed.

The team was transported over to the hotel by bus and by the time they checked into their rooms, it was well after midnight and the players were due for an eight am skate even though the game wasn't until the next day.

Seraphina had given Brandon a copy of their room key but didn't make any plans with him on whether he would come up or not. That was entirely up to him and she wasn't going to wait around and figure it out. Even when Katella asked whether Thorpe would be here, Seraphina answered honestly: "I don't know."

"Negan is," Katella said. She gave her sister a long look. "I'm here if you need me, Sera."

Seraphina nodded once. "Thanks," she said.

Just as she was dozing off, however, Seraphina heard the door to her room click open and the soft, familiar footsteps of Brandon. Through slitted eyes, she could see his tall figure crawl onto the bed, could feel his large hand cup her cheek, and then he gave her a long, slow kiss.

"I didn't think you would come," she murmured in a sleepy voice.

"And resist being next to you?" he asked. "I've been wanting to do this for over a year and a half. We have a lot of time to make up for."

He gave her a long, lasting kiss, sending shockwaves through her system and making her knees go weak. Thank goodness she was lying down or else she would have fallen off-balance like a clutz.

"Wait," he murmured against her lips. "Wait, wait, wait. We

have to talk about this, Seraphina. I want you... I want to be inside you. Fuck, I want you. But I can't just... I won't." He stopped and looked her in the eye. She could tell by the clenched jaw and the hard eyes that it took a lot out of him just to control himself. He wanted her just like she wanted him, and it took everything in her to resist him, to hold back from seducing him - because she knew if she kissed his neck and caressed his body he would succumb and save the talking for later - because she knew this was important to him. And if it was important to him, it should be important to her as well.

"Okay," she agreed with a nod of her head. "What would you like to talk about?"

"Us," he said as though it was the most obvious thing in the world. "I want to talk about me and you and what this is. My feelings haven't changed, Sera. If we're going to do this, I want to do this right. I'm not going to half-ass this. I want you completely. I don't want you with anyone else. I don't want you only to have sex with you. I want to be in a relationship with you where we hold hands and have sex and make plans. I can't do anything less."

Seraphina bit her bottom lip and nodded. "I know," she told him. "I've been giving this a lot of thought. And I agree. But we can't go public, Brandon. Not right now. Maybe not for a while. I would need to talk to my lawyer and make sure we're covered legally. And if we're not, we might have to keep our relationship a secret for a while. For however long I'm owner of the team or you're on my team."

"But you would be with me?" he asked. "I know it's under-cover, we have to hide things for a while, but you would still be with me?"

"Of course, Brandon," she said, looking at him with wonder. "I want to be with you out in public. But would you be willing to wait for that?" She wasn't sure if this was going to work at all but she was willing to try.

"I'd do anything for you," he told her sincerely. "Just as long as we got-"

Now it was her turn to shut him up with a kiss.

Brandon Thorpe didn't have many friends. Truth be told, he didn't have any friends. Even his own teammates didn't socialize with him much, and he was their captain. Of course, he didn't take it personally. He understood that he hadn't actually put himself out there so it wouldn't make sense for them to make the effort when it was his responsibility to reach out and contribute in some way as well.

He didn't particularly care one way or the other. He knew that out on the ice, his team had his back, regardless of how they personally felt about him. It was what you did when you were on a team: you had your team's back no matter what.

Well, most of his teammates had that mentality. Negan and Matt Peters, Katella's ex, didn't get along and Negan hadn't gone out of his way to pretend he liked the guy. Although, if Brandon was being honest, he couldn't really blame Negan. Peters had run his mouth – which wasn't like him – about Katella and Negan protected his girl, regardless of who was doing the talking. Negan wasn't the sort of man to subscribe to the philosophy of bros before hos, and Brandon had to respect him for it. Brandon was also against that adage because he grew up with women – a mother and a sister. If anyone ran their mouth about them, he would have no problem putting them in their place no matter who said it.

"Hey." Thorpe picked his head up from the ice, looking over to see Negan standing by his goal post, nodding at him. Because it was a light practice, he wasn't wearing his helmet.

"Hey," Brandon acknowledged in return.

"How're you doing?"

Brandon cut Negan a sideways look. It wasn't as though he was suspicious of Negan's motives, per se, but at the same time, Negan wasn't the sort of guy to talk if he didn't want to talk.

He'd always been cordial and respectful with Brandon – and a lot of that might have had to do with the fact that Brandon was captain – but Negan never skated over during a quick break of morning skate to ask how he was.

"In regards to?" Brandon asked, hoping it didn't come out like he was being a smartass. Because that definitely wasn't his intention.

"Your hand," Negan said, glancing at Brandon's right hand. "You beat the shit out of Stevens."

"The guy deserved it," Brandon said. Technically speaking, he shouldn't be practicing right now. And he really wasn't. But he at least wanted to skate with the pads on, keep his legs fresh, practice holding his stick even with the pain.

"They always do," Negan agreed with a nod, crossing his arms over his chest. "Look, I'm going to get straight to the point. You don't really talk that much and you kind of come across like a dick. But you're my captain and after what happened last night, I want you to know I have your back."

Brandon glanced over at him. "You didn't have to tell me that," he said. "I know you guys do."

"Look, I'm not really good at this whole talking thing," he said. Brandon glanced over at him, his lips curled up into a gentle smirk. "But I just want you to know, I really respect what you did out there. Yeah, you fought and we fight in hockey. But I was out on the ice when Stevens was running his mouth, and if you hadn't jumped in and taken care of him, I would have. He shouldn't be talking about Seraphina that way. It's such bullshit."

"You sound like you understand," Brandon pointed out.

Negan snorted, crossing his arms over his chest and looked down, shaking his head. There was a wry smile on his face before he picked his eyes up and looking at Brandon. "I don't talk much," he said again, "but I figure you're in the same place as I am. Dating a Hanson sister is not a walk in the park, let me tell you."

Brandon pushed his brows up. "That fight," he said, "when you went off on Guzman."

Negan nodded. "Guilty," he said. "The guy was running his mouth about Kat to Peters, Peters wasn't doing shit. I'm not talking bad about my team, but Jesus, that's your owner, kind of. You know? Even though you broke up, she's still part of your family. You defend her."

"It doesn't look like Peters needed to defend her," Brandon pointed out. "Not when she had you."

"Like I said," Negan said. "I know what you're going through."

Brandon gave him a look from the corner of his eyes. "Are you here to tell me that you understand but we should still be putting the team first since we're so close to a guaranteed playoff spot?" he asked, furrowing his brow.

Negan tilted his head to the side. "Absolutely not," he said. "If anything, I'm the opposite. That's not to say that I wouldn't put the team first, but if someone talks about my girl in a particular way, whether or not he's only trying to get in my head, I'm going to make him realize he can't fucking talk about her that way, you know?"

Brandon nodded once but didn't say anything. He understood where Negan was coming from. He lost it, just like Negan did. The difference was, Negan was known for being an instigator. He was known for running his mouth and trying to get the other team's players off the ice in order to get an advantage. Ironically enough, Guzman hadn't even targeted Negan. Negan just reacted, which meant Guzman must have been saying some pretty bad things about Katella. Brandon couldn't blame him.

"The problem is, you've put a target on your back," Negan continued, looking at him with serious brown eyes. "If other teams know how you feel about her, they're going to try and get you off the ice. We can't have you off the ice. We're a good team but you've kept us in games we should have lost. We need you. So if anyone runs his mouth about Seraphina again, just let me know and I've got him, okay? I'd rather sit for five than lose you for the whole game. I don't want to risk it."

Brandon was surprised by Negan's comments. He nodded his head, trying to cover up that surprise.

"Thanks, man," he said.

Negan nodded. "Sure," he said, sticking out his gloved hand.

Brandon tapped it with his own.

"Just so you know," Brandon said quickly. "The team is better because you're on it."

Negan gave him a wolfish grin. "I think that that's the nicest thing you've ever said to me," he said. "In fact, I think that that's the only thing you've really said to me."

Brandon chuckled. "I guess I'll have to work on that," he said.

Chapter 15

HOUSTON WAS HOT AND STICKY, even in late February. Because the team arrived late at night, the majority of them went to bed. A few single guys decided to check out the nightlife, which was fine, just as long as they showed up tomorrow to play. Seraphina got two suites, one for her and Katella, the other for Emma and Harper. Emma researched what they could do in Houston in case their boyfriends wanted rest or time to themselves before the game and managed to find a small fair a few miles south of where the rink was located.

After breakfast that morning with Brandon at her side, kissing her shoulders and placing his hand on her thigh, Seraphina pulled him into the shower with her so he could scrub her down and bend her over and take her from behind as the warm water hit their backs and muffled their moaning. Perhaps it wasn't the smartest decision to have sex without protection but Seraphina was on birth control and she knew Brandon didn't have any STDs thanks to yearly testing all the players had to submit to.

He carried her to her bed and they fell asleep together for a long nap.

When they woke up, Katella was banging on their door. Brandon grunted and Seraphina groaned. She was ready to throw her pillow at her sister and shout at her to leave her alone.

"We're going out to dinner," Katella said through the closed door. "Wanna come?" Seraphina opened her mouth to respond when Katella cut her off. "And don't be gross."

Seraphina laughed. "Isn't that the pot calling the kettle black?" she teased. She glanced over at Brandon, still dozing, so beautiful in the shadows. There would be plenty of time to come out publicly. Right now, she wanted to keep this to themselves for as long as they could. "We're ordering room service, but thanks."

"Ah, I remember those days," Katella murmured from the other side of the door. "Never leaving the room, getting acquainted with each other."

"You literally started dating Negan a month ago," Seraphina called causing Brandon to chuckle from behind her.

She turned to stare at him. The lower half of his body was covered with hotel blankets while his chest and arms were completely bare for her to stare at, to take in. He was beautiful, it almost hurt to look at him.

They ordered room service and indulged once more in intimate behavior. When their food came, Brandon met the waiter at the door and wheeled the table in himself so Seraphina didn't have to worry about a stranger seeing her naked. They turned on the television and flipped through the channels until Brandon put it on the NHL network. They were replaying a recap of all the games that had happened for the day, including any tidbits and hockey news that came out.

Seraphina took a rather unladylike bite of her spaghetti before nearly choking on her food. Phil Bambridge was being interviewed after the game the Blackjacks had with the Gulls'.

"I couldn't say why Brandon Thorpe dropped gloves," he pointed out, shrugging his shoulders as he stood at the podium, looking out at a group of reporters. Seraphina scrunched her brow. She hadn't realized she had been expected to say something after the game. But then she realized that this press conference was likely called by Bambridge himself. And her heart started to pound against her chest like a clock chiming out the time in heavy steady beats. "But I can speculate. I mean, you know players, right? They get under your skin anyway they can, right? And if they get you off the ice, it's golden. And that's awesome. And that's what Stevens did. He did his job. I didn't think he would take out Thorpe, though. I mean, he's steely and focused and he's never off his game, you know?"

"He didn't answer the question," Seraphina muttered to herself, rolling her eyes.

"Yes, but what did Stevens say to disgruntle Thorpe so much?" the reporter asked.

"Did you ask Stevens?" Bambridge asked, scratching the back of his head. "And he didn't say anything? Well, it's not my place to say or to guess, you know? But it might have to do with the fact that his GM and I had dinner plans that he didn't agree with."

"You asked Seraphina Hanson on a date?" someone else called.

Seraphina felt her cheeks turn pink and Brandon tensed behind her. Even though she wasn't staring at Brandon, she could feel him narrow his eyes at the screen.

"No, no," he said, though his smile was arrogant. "I made myself very clear. I don't know how she interpreted it but I wanted to get to know all GMs. I'm the new kid in the block, you know? I'm networking." He clapped his hands together and looked away before finding a camera and smiling. "But it wouldn't surprise me if she interpreted it that way. I mean, she wore this amazing white dress that left nothing to the imagination, if you know what I mean. God, she's gorgeous. Have you seen her? I mean, if that was my boss, I'd be protective of her too."

"Are you insinuating Thorpe punched Stevens because

Stevens said something about Seraphina Hanson?" somebody shouted at him.

Bambridge shrugged his shoulders but a telling smile stayed on his face.

"Like I said," he said with a shrug. "Who am I to say? I'm not going to question my guys with what gets said on the ice. That's why I have Connelly on the bench, coaching them. That's his job. But, let's be real. This is the first female owner slash manager the NHL has seen. It wouldn't surprise me in the least if feelings should happen to get involved. She's been around hockey her whole life, you know? Her sister's dated at least one player we know of and she's rumored to have hooked up with another. Hell, she's probably dating someone new, probably a Gull, now, too."

He took a minute to pause and Seraphina clenched her jaw so tightly so thought she might pop a brain vessel. Who did he think he was, talking about her sister like that? Like he knew her. He didn't know anything about them. But just because they were female, he could speak that way about them. Would he say that about the GM from any of the Canadian teams? For the Hollywood and Sacramento teams?

Of course he wouldn't. This was plain sexism and now Katella was involved and she hadn't done anything wrong.

"This is all pure speculation," another reporter – a female – pointed out. "Katella Hanson has nothing to do with the original question of Stevens instigating a fight with Brandon Thorpe."

"Technically speaking," Bambridge said, glancing at the female reporter and giving her a charm smile. "Thorpe started the fight."

"With all due respect, Mr. Bambridge," she said. "It's clear Stevens said something and continued to say something until Thorpe was provoked. I know you're new here but Brandon Thorpe doesn't lose control like he did out there on the ice.

Something had to have riled him up for him to respond that way."

"How do you know it was what Stevens said?" Bambridge asked, the charm smile gone from his face. He gripped the podium so his knuckles were white and his eyes narrowed in her direction. "How do you know it wasn't the fact that Seraphina Hanson agreed to go to dinner with me and he got jealous?"

There was a moment of silence. Literally, a beat of complete stillness in the room where everyone present needed time to process what Bambridge just said.

"Are you insinuating that Brandon Thorpe has feelings for Seraphina Hanson?" the female reporter asked. She sounded familiar but Seraphina couldn't place the voice.

"Do you know if Seraphina Hanson has engaged in illicit behavior with her player?" another correspondent shouted.

"Or maybe he's just being protective of his team's owner?" someone else said.

"Why would Stevens even talk about Seraphina Hanson?" another reporter asked. "I highly doubt he's going to talk about another GM that way. Wouldn't that reveal misogynistic tendencies?"

"Whoa, whoa, whoa," Bambridge said, putting his hands up in a sort of defensive gesture. "When did this suddenly become a *let's attack Stevens* line of questions? Look, it doesn't matter whether or not Stevens said anything about Seraphina Hanson. What matters is the retaliation. A goalie - a calm, stoic goalie targeted my player, threatened him to fight, and had to be pried away from Stevens. Don't you think that that should be questioned? We never see goalies fighting. Patrick Roy isn't playing anymore, as far as I know. Is there something going on between Thorpe and Hanson? Possibly. Like I said, she was all over me at our date to the point where I had to remind her that this was a business meeting. I mean, yeah, she's gorgeous, don't get me wrong, but I'm here because I'm a professional. I'm not going to sleep with my fellow GMs in order to try and attain certain players."

"What?" Seraphina asked in a flat yelp.

Brandon dropped his glass of soda on the carpeted floor, spilling the dark bubbly liquid everywhere. He clenched his jaw so tightly there was a good chance he was going to cause a hemorrhage somewhere.

"That's extremely libelous," the female reporter pointed out.

"It's not libelous if it's true, sweetheart," Phil said in a condescending tone.

"So you're telling me Seraphina Hanson made advances on you and you rejected her?" the reporter asked. "Aren't you the same man who got arrested twice for assaulting two different women?"

"What does my history have anything to do with this press conference?" Phil asked.

"What do Seraphina's looks have anything to do with her job?"

Phil made a face. "You know what?" he asked. "I'm over the feminist bullshit. I'm here to talk about what happened between Thorpe and Stevens. Do I think the fighting was excessive? Hell yeah, I do. Stevens hit the ice and Thorpe managed to get a couple of punches in while he was on the ice. That's cheap."

"So is making sexual remarks about his GM," the reporter said. "You can call it feminist bullshit all you want, Phil, but the truth of the matter is Stevens - if he did speak about Seraphina Hanson at all - would never talk about another GM the way he talked about Seraphina Hanson. That implies her sex has something to do with it."

"Of course it does!" Phil said. "Why would he talk about a male GM?"

"Do you deny there are gay hockey players?"

Phil pinched the bridge of his nose. "Who are you again?" he asked.

"Harper Crawford," she replied.

Seraphina had never been more proud of Harper than she was right now. Tears had sprung into her eyes and she was so grateful to have her friendship.

"Aren't you dating Zachary Ryan?" he asked. "You're the blogger for the Gulls', right? So your view is already skewed. Of course you would defend Brandon Thorpe."

"Brandon Thorpe isn't even going to get suspended," Harper pointed out. "Are you really standing up here, upset that a fight broke out at a hockey game between two opposing players?"

Phil glared. "I think we're done here," he said, and before anyone could say anything else, he stomped off stage.

"Thank God for Harper," Seraphina murmured to herself.

"He's lucky I'm in another state right now," Brandon said.

Seraphina glanced over at him as she turned off the television. "Don't worry about it," she said. "Seriously." She placed her lips on his and gave him a long kiss. "I can think of a way to distract ourselves."

"Can you?" He raised his brows.

She laughed and kissed him again.

Chapter 16

SERAPHINA ATTENDED the game the next day with Katella, Harper, and Emma. She bought glass seats like she had last game and even though she and her sister were recognized by some of the Houston fans, who weren't above calling them derogatory names as they walked through the stadium, they all held their heads high. Seraphina felt her eyes pinch with unshed tears but she refused to let them fall. Not in front of these people. Not in front of her team. She had to project strength and impassiveness even though she wanted nothing more than to break down and cry.

To be honest, she had no idea how Katella was keeping it together. Currently, she was joking with Harper while taking a long swig of her overpriced water bottle. Phil Bambridge ripped her a new one last night and Katella hadn't even been involved in what happened. She was furious that he would talk about Seraphina that way, just because she called him out on his misogynistic tendencies and said no to his advances, but to bring Katella into it, like she had anything to do with it, infuriated her even more.

And now, she had people attacking her like they knew her,

like they had any idea what was going on. The worst part about this whole thing was the fact that she couldn't even come out with the entire truth about what had happened between her and Bambridge because she would look like a spiteful, vindictive bitch if she did. Plus, she couldn't prove anything because it was he-said, she-said. He felt her up. He didn't leave a mark on her. Even if she did, people wouldn't believe her. Why would they, when Phil Bambridge was attractive and charming and didn't say things he should say? Why was he allowed to be quirky and different and get praised for it when, if she had done the same thing, she would get ridiculed and criticized?

The girls headed to their seats while Seraphina decided to head to the locker room. She had something she needed to say to the team. She just needed to get a hold of her emotions first.

Seraphina took some deep breaths as she took the elevator down to the lower level. The elevator attendant wouldn't even look at her. Perfect. People judged her who didn't even know her. Nobody thought to even ask her for her side of the story. Why would they? Why would anyone believe her? It was clear she was just some typical female immersed in a man's world. She had no other option but to either fall in love or act like a dumbass.

The problem was, technically, she had done both. When she first inherited the team, she knew next to nothing about hockey. She researched her butt off until she felt somewhat familiar with all the terminology and the sport – the history, the rules, the strategies, the positions, the attitudes, everything.

And then, she fell in love with her captain. It wasn't as though she tried; it just happened. He drew her to him with his stoic, brooding presence, his quiet demeanor. She was attracted to the fact that he didn't need to speak in order to prove anything. All he needed to do was let his skill speak for himself, and it did when he was nominated for the Vezna last year, despite their shitty season.

She remembered that night. She wound up attending the

awards ceremony because her player was nominated. He hadn't taken anyone and neither had she but they had only spoken a few words - her congratulating him, him thanking her.

How could they have wasted so much time? She shook her head as she headed into the locker room. It didn't matter; they were together now and that was all that was important.

When she walked in, the players turned to look at her. She paused, suddenly stricken by their probing gazes. And then, someone started to clap. Seraphina didn't know who it was but soon everyone was clapping and she climbed onto the bench so she could be seen with ease. She managed to find Brandon, looking good in his tan suit and somewhat brushed hair. He wouldn't be playing tonight because of his injury so Jimmy Stafford was suited up and they had to fly in a backup for Stafford from their Irvine AHL team. He gave her a small smile, causing her heart to flutter. He didn't say much but she knew he supported her, that he stood behind her, no matter what.

"Um, thanks?" she said, cocking her head once everyone had finished clapping. "If we are clapping for anyone, it should be Katella. She didn't deserve any of what Bambridge was spewing last night. Also Harper." Her eyes found Zach's and she pushed her brows up, letting him know just how impressed she was with him. "She was a badass and held her ground with Bambridge. I'm glad she's in our corner. Not to put you on blast or anything, but don't fuck that up."

"Trust me, I know," Zach said with his usual boyish smile.

Her eyes found Negan and she saw how black his eyes were, how his teeth were clenched together, how his entire body was rigid with fury. Even though it had nearly been twenty-four hours and he had seen her since then, Seraphina could tell how angry he was with what happened. Hell, she was too.

"I'm here because as I'm sure you already know, Phil Bambridge is a liar," she said. "I definitely don't sleep with people to get players and there was no bone in my body that wanted to sleep with him, out of all people. I don't want this to take away what our focus is and should be about - winning and getting to playoffs. That's my concern."

"What happened between you and Bambridge?" somebody asked. Seraphina wasn't able to see who.

"That's no one's business," Brandon said before she could answer.

Seraphina restrained herself from giving Brandon a look that said she could handle herself. He was just trying to protect her.

"It doesn't matter," she said gently. "What matters is, none of it is true."

"We know that," Alec Schumacher said, first line winger with Zachary Ryan and Kyle Underwood. "But we want to know if you're okay. If anything happened, Seraphina, you could always file a police report, just to get something documented."

Seraphina smiled brightly at Alec. He had changed so much over the years. The two of them were roughly the same age and she remembered when her grandfather used to take her and her sister to his Triple A hockey games, back when the three of them were in high school. Katella had a little crush on him, despite the fact that she was a couple of years older than he was and typically had a thing for older guys. He was charming and good looking with dark blond hair and blue eyes – very Southern California-esque – but he had a reputation of dating supermodels and Gulls Girls and never had a steady girlfriend. When Katella told her he wouldn't be bringing a plus one to the AllStar Auction last month, Seraphina was surprised. In fact, now that she thought about it, he hadn't been seen with anyone in a year. Hell, he hadn't even been flirting with any Girls.

Katella thought this meant he was dating someone – probably a Girl – but Seraphina wasn't too sure. Everyone knew the rule about dating – *A rule you're breaking yourself if you're with Brandon Thorpe,* a voice pointed out – and how players and Gulls Girls weren't allowed to socialize outside the ice rink. He was also getting older and that could mean he was getting more mature.

"Yeah, I'd rather not get that involved with this," she said. "Plus, if I did file a police report, the public would be able to get a hold of it and that's the last thing I want."

Drew Stefano, second line winger and the fastest skater on the team tentatively raised his hand. "Actually, that isn't true," he said. "I majored in Criminology at the University of Michigan while I was there and interned at a police department. Police reports aren't actually public record. Certain things are, yes, like date, time, location, but what actually happened and personal identifiers don't have to be released by the department if that's their policy."

Seraphina nodded. Drew Stefano was one of the few skaters on the team that chose to attend college after being drafted by Edmonton. He was short, five foot nine, but lean and muscled, with olive skin, dark eyes and brown hair. Very Italian. He had speed and had the most short-handed goals in the league – five for now.

"Good to know," she said. "I could totally see Bambridge grabbing a copy and making it public record by turning it over to the media or some other bullshit like that."

"Are you all right?" Dimitri Petrov's voice came from the back of the crowd, and when Seraphina looked at him, her heart did a little flip. He was too beautiful for his own good. It made no sense why his wife was leaving him – when she was the one who cheated on him in the first place! They had been married for ten years, with two children, seven and four. Seraphina hated that their family was broken up because of her poor decisions and her selfishness. Dimitri was one of the most loyal hockey players she had ever known. His ex-wife was lucky to have him.

"Yeah, actually," Seraphina said with a nod of her head. "I am. I just want to tell you that tonight and every night, actually, the game isn't about me. Teams – especially teams that are clamoring for a playoff spot just like we are or teams that definitely won't make playoffs and are bitter about it – will do anything they can to prevent us from winning the game. If they're going down, they're going down swinging and they're going to try and take out as many of us as they can." She began to make eye contact with each player. "Don't let them take you down. Don't let them take you out. We are so close, guys. We are so close to a playoff spot that I can taste it. Can't you?"

The team nodded their heads. Some chose to remain still preferring to listen rather than respond.

"They are going to do and say whatever they can to try and get you off the ice," Seraphina continued. "They could talk about your mothers and sisters, your girlfriends and your wives. They could say the worst kind of things you do not want to hear about them because they're trying to get a reaction out of you. See, I always thought that there were lines of the code of hockey and fighting. But when a team gets desperate, there aren't. Kind of like real life. Recognize it for what it is but don't engage.

"The only exception to that is if you're fighting as part of a strategy. Don't let some fourth-line goon get you off the ice for five minutes. If you're trying to take out a skilled player or if you're trying to send a message because some asshole checks Onni and the hit is maybe too high, by all means, go for it."

A couple of the players chuckled and Zachary Ryan nudged the young defenseman with his shoulder.

"They're going to try," Seraphina said seriously. "Especially with what happened with Brandon. Phil Bambridge is an idiot. Stevens was running his mouth and Brandon did something about it. I mean, how kickass is that, that our goalie got into fight? Maybe soon, he'll get a Gordie Howe hat trick."

More chuckles and Alec Schumacher whistled.

"I want what's best for the team," she said, a smile on her face. "And that means not letting these assholes get under your skin. And they'll try. Just do what you need to do. You don't have to prove anything. Your skill already does that. We have arguably one of the best teams in the league. Sure, it's been a struggle to actually get where we are now, but who cares? We're here, and that's because of the effort you all put in day in, day out. Whether you're working out in the off-season and skating during the summer, whether you're swearing off alcohol or partying or whatever, you're making sacrifices for the team. I am so proud of our group here and I don't want you to think you need to defend me or my sister or anyone for that matter. This isn't about us. It's about *you*. So go out there and play on. That's it. Play. And win. The best revenge is making playoffs and proving them wrong. Okay?"

"You guys can do this," Brandon said, stepping forward. He rarely spoke so the crowd was surprised. "We can do this. Go out there and win. What do you say?"

So they did.

Chapter 17

THE NEWPORT SEAGULLS ended up beating Houston 1-0. It was a gritty game that started since puck drop in the first period. Seraphina had no idea who she was kidding when she gave her speech but she wanted to make sure her voice was heard and that the team knew what their number one priority was: get the two points. Houston was going to do everything in their power to try and throw off their game. They were going to talk about Seraphina, Katella, and any other woman close to the team in order to get a reaction. Things were already tense, and for some reason, the Gulls seemed to have a chip on their shoulder.

Somehow, no one got kicked out of the game. Negan did get into a fight when a fourth liner who checked one of the Gulls' rookie defenseman a little too hard in the corner and there was no call.

Katella, of course, jumped up and cheered, especially when Negan managed to knock the fourth liner on his ass. Both team benches had the players banging their sticks against the outside wall of their bench, showing support for their teammate.

Brandon didn't play due to his hand still needing to heal

after what happened two nights ago in Vegas. He wasn't on the bench with his teammates. Due to his injury, he wore a suit and was up in the press box. They had to call a backup from their Irvine AHL team and fly Sam Jones over from John Wayne just in case he had to start. Luckily, Jimmy Stafford was on point and he managed to keep them in the game, earning his first-ever NHL shutout. Seraphina couldn't stop smiling for the kid. When he was announced as the game's number one star, she cheered for him. He deserved it.

Instead of partying right away, they had to hop a quick flight from Houston to Phoenix. They got there just after eleven at night. Everyone checked in and – Seraphina hoped – stayed in and got sleep. They were ten points shy of an actual seeded playoff spot and that was if the Sacramento Suns lost every single game. She wanted everyone on their game because they needed all the points they could get. If they won the next three games, it was all but guaranteed that they would clinch a wild-card spot, but Seraphina wanted the seed. She wanted the safety.

They checked into a comfortable hotel a couple of blocks from the Phoenix rink, which happened to be right next to an outdoor mall. By the time they made it to their rooms, Katella changed into one of Negan's old shirts and passed out on her bed. Seraphina wasn't sure if Negan would come in later or if they decided they needed a break to catch up on sleeping, but minutes after, Brandon came to the door and crawled into bed with her.

"How's your hand?" she whispered in the darkness. Katella's bed was in the next room but she was a light sleeper so Seraphina made sure to keep things quiet.

"Better." He raised his right hand and began to curl and flex his fingers. "Not one hundred percent but I'm playing tomorrow."

"Do you think you should?" Seraphina asked, furrowing her

brow. "Not that you're incapable. I just want to make sure you don't make it worse. Especially with playoffs."

"Do you trust me?" he asked her. He wasn't defensive but there was something in his eyes that seemed insistent that she be honest.

"Of course I do," she told him, as though it was the most obvious thing in the world. She reached up and cupped his cheek with her hand. "Of course I trust you, Brandon. I know you can do anything, really. But I don't want you to let your pride get in the way of what's best for the team."

"Do you think I would put pride before the team?" he asked, quirking a brow.

"You don't bond with your team at all," she pointed out. "You don't encourage your backup much."

"That makes me unsocial, not prideful."

"Either way, you're putting what you want before what they need," she pointed out. "Did you even tell Stafford what a great job he did last night?" She pressed her brows up, emphasizing her point. "Come on, Brandon. You're captain. This is part of your job. And your hand hurts but you're not even considering maybe sitting out."

"Because I know I can do this, Seraphina," he said, his voice insistent. "If anyone knows me, it's me. I know I can do it. If I didn't think I could, I wouldn't do it. I promise you, I wouldn't."

Seraphina looked into his eyes and considered what he was saying for a long moment. This was the conflict of interest. This was the hard part. If the player was anyone else, she would have told them to take one more game just to be sure. But this was Brandon and he was her exception to everything. Everything. Even if they weren't dating, even if they weren't together, she would have left the decision up to him.

"Okay," she said with one nod.

"Okay?" he asked, somewhat surprised. He thought she was going to fight him more on this. She was almost offended that he would make that assumption.

"Okay," she said again. "I trust you. If you think you can do it, I believe you."

He smiled. She still wasn't used to his smile and she was mesmerized by it. She couldn't help but tilt her chin up so she could kiss his lips and run her fingers through his hair. It was soft and made her sigh through the kiss.

"I love you," she breathed out before she could stop herself.

He pulled back, surprised even more. His green eyes were narrowed, trying to read her face, trying to decipher if she was being honest. Her cheeks turned red now, not fully believing that she had actually said that to him so early in their relationship – even though she had told him as much after their first night together.

"What did you say?" Brandon asked. His voice was touched with awe and wonder, almost as though he didn't believe what he had heard.

"I love you," she repeated again.

He smiled then, a beaming smile that completely filled his face with light and crinkled his eyes and made him the most beautiful thing she had ever seen on this earth.

"I love you too," he told her.

And she believed him. She could read his eyes and he actually spoke the words and Brandon Thorpe never said anything he didn't mean. He didn't say much of anything at all. But he said he loved her. And that made it true.

He took her face in his hands and gave her a long, slow kiss. She opened her mouth and he immediately responded, sliding his tongue into her mouth and kissing her like the world was burning around them but all he could concentrate on was this kiss and exploring her mouth like this was his last opportunity to do so. She loved the feel of his hands on her face as he gently took control of the kiss. She could feel his strength in his hands and that feeling of restrained power caused her pelvis to thrum with tightness.

She crawled on top of him, straddling his waist without

breaking their kiss. She could feel his hardness press against the inside of her thigh. Even though they had gotten extremely familiar with each other, sometimes multiple times in one day, Seraphina still felt a rush of excitement, knowing that he wanted her, knowing that she brought him to such pleasure that just kissing got him hard.

Seraphina pressed against his hardness and he groaned through the kiss, his grip on her face tightening.

She gasped. She loved having this sort of power over him. She wanted to feel him move and writhe against her. She wanted to hear her name on his lips.

His hands slid under her shirt, cupping her back before sliding her shirt over her head and dropping it to the floor. He ran his cool hands over her soft skin and she shuddered at the conflicting sensation. She locked her arms behind his neck and spread her legs wider for him, deepening the kiss even further. She pulled his own shirt off and started attacking his neck with her mouth, her teeth, her lips. She loved running her fingers up and down his torso, feeling the muscles twitch and spasm underneath her touch.

More clothing was shed and discarded. Seraphina positioned herself in his lap once she was completely naked and she took his cock in her hand while her left hand gripped his shoulder. He groaned and shuddered under her touch. She began to stroke him in long, fluid strokes, up and down. Each time she did, he twitched underneath her. His head was thrown back against the pillows. He looked beautiful in the glow of the moon seeping through the windows.

She spread her thighs for him and proceeded to lower herself onto his cock. She hissed as he pushed through her folds and coated him with her slickness. She had always loved having sex but she had never been with anyone who caused her to get wet with just a look, an innocent touch. Even something as savage as fighting the way he had back in Vegas made her pelvis throb and she held back a groan.

"Don't you dare," he murmured, his eyes at half-mast. "I want to hear you scream for me."

Once she got used to his size, Seraphina began to move up and down Brandon's hard cock, trying to get as much of him inside of her as she could. His hands gripped her hips as she did so, holding her in place. His mouth found her nipples and he began to suck on them as she moved, causing her to cry out and speed up. His grip on her tightened now that he knew what she liked and he continued to suck and tease and even gently nibble on the sensitive pink nubs until she started to quicken her breathing, until it was hard for her to continue to move since the buildup was starting to get too intense.

Her hands found his shoulders and she sunk her nails into his flesh. He let out a groan. "Sera," he managed to get out. "I need you to come now because I am and there's no way for me to stop it."

His words were her undoing and when she released herself, he did as well. Seraphina had never thought it was possible to actually come with someone, at the same time. It had never happened to her and she just assumed it was one of those Hollywood legends that she read about in books or saw on television that didn't actually happen in reality.

But she was wrong and she was so glad she was because she had never thought an orgasm could feel like *this*. Orgasms were the most selfish things she had ever felt in her body due to the fact that they were all about her. But when it happened with someone else, there was something special, something that bonded the two together, something she was so lucky she got to experience with Brandon.

"Jesus," he murmured, his forehead hitting her shoulders as he began to soften inside of her. His hands released her hips and circled around her waist. Seraphina placed her head on top of his and began to lightly scratch his back with her fingernails.

She chuckled. "I feel the same way," she murmured.

"That feels good," he said, indicating her scratching.

"I'm glad," she murmured. "I'm glad you're with me. I don't know what I'd do without you."

"You would survive, Sera," Brandon told her, picking his head up and locking eyes with her. "Sometimes, I think you forget how strong you are. You think you need someone else to guide you – me, your grandfather. But you don't need us. You can do this on your own. I believe in you."

Seraphina felt her heart clench. She had never thought about it that way before. She gripped his face in her hands and kissed him long and slow. She could feel him stir underneath her and she smirked.

Perhaps he was right. But it was nice knowing she had him in her corner.

Chapter 18

WHEN THE TEAM finally returned back to Newport Beach, they said their goodbyes and headed home for the night. Brandon decided that he needed to check on his home and they would meet the next morning after morning skate for brunch. Seraphina was glad for the space. It had been an overwhelming past few days and she never really had a moment to process what had happened. She kept a strong front up when she was around everyone, including Brandon and Katella. She didn't want them worrying about her when Brandon needed to focus on winning, on the game, and Katella needed to focus on her own life and quite possibly Negan. She needed to keep her feelings to herself because she didn't want them worrying about her.

Plus, she knew what was she was getting into when she accepted the offer her grandfather had laid out in his will and trust.

Actually, no. That was a lie. She had no idea what it really took to run a hockey team as a young female. But she had a decision to make and there was no way she was going to sell the team, no matter how badly her uncles wanted to. This was her grandfather's legacy and she wasn't going to give that up, especially after he entrusted it to her.

When she got to her bedroom, she threw on her pajamas and crawled into bed. She grabbed a picture frame, sitting on her nightstand. It was one of her grandfather's official photos of himself, his last year before he was murdered by his accountant. She liked keeping him close. It made her feel safe.

Without warning, tears accumulated in her eyes and started to fall. She knew these were the ones she had been holding back the past couple of days. Now that she was finally alone, now that she was holding a picture of her grandfather, she was finally free to cry. Her door was closed and she and Katella had rooms on the opposite ends of the house so Seraphina highly doubted Katella would even be able to hear her cry.

She didn't try to stop herself, didn't try to hide it. She clutched the picture to her chest and hugged it like she was hugging him, like he hadn't been taken from her too early, like he was still here with her, comforting her. She hated that he was gone. She hated that she couldn't go to him for advice the same way she used to when he was alive. She hated that he couldn't pat her on the back and tell her everything was going to be all right.

After a good fifteen minutes, she felt the sobs slowly begin to stop. The tears started to dry up, leaving her eyes sore and red. The snot was quickly rubbed away from underneath her nose with the back of her hand. Her hands still held the picture but her grip wasn't as desperately tight.

A calm settled over her, like everything was okay. Everything would be okay. Phil Bambridge could run his mouth as much as he wanted to but that wouldn't change anything. She still owned the team. Her team would probably make playoffs, his definitely would not. He was lashing out, attacking the weakest link, and due to her gender, that weak link was her. But that could also be her strength. She was going to call him out on his bullshit but she needed to figure out how. She needed to figure out how to do it in a way where she wasn't playing his game, where she wasn't taking cheap shots and making accusations where she could bring a defamation lawsuit against him.

At that moment, her phone chirped.

You awake?

Seraphina felt her lips curl into a smile at Brandon's text. She responded with, *I can't sleep.*

Neither can I. It feels strange to have a bed to myself again.

Seraphina felt her cheeks turn red and warmth blossomed in her chest.

I don't like it, he sent her. **I would rather share one with you.**

I miss you, too, she texted him. And she did.

Brunch tomorrow?

She smiled. It was nice to be missed. It was nice to be texted first. It was nice to be in a relationship with someone she loved.

Wouldn't miss it for the world.

WHEN SHE WOKE up the next morning, Seraphina was still holding onto her grandfather's photo. She smiled as she stretched. Today was a new day. Today would be better than yesterday. She stepped into her shower and turned on hot water, letting the beads of water drop in her naked body and wash away any trace of tears and sadness and loss from yesterday. It woke her up and helped sharpen her focus. She had a few more days before the trade deadline and she wanted to see if there were any defenseman she could up pick up without sacrificing the core players on her team. She might be willing to part with a couple of draft picks depending on who was offered and how badly she needed them.

She blew her hair dry and pinned the bangs back before slipping on a navy blue dress with a matching belt she tied around her waist. She wore simple black heels and a white cardigan sweater due to the cold the morning promised.

Seraphina insisted that they meet at the Stuft Surfer, a diner on the beach, just off of Fifteenth Street. She loved that this mom-and-pop place was open, even when it wasn't tourist season and the beach was still somewhat empty, even at ten o'clock in the morning. It was cold this morning. There wasn't a cloud in the sky. It was clear blue, however, so she didn't think it would rain today, although this weekend promised some drizzles here and there. She managed to find a place to park on the street that didn't require paying, even if it was a block away. Seraphina didn't actually mind walking in heels but she avoided it when she could.

She would not be able to at the beach.

Brandon was already there, sitting at one of the benches just outside the diner, placed in the sand. When he saw her, he stood and strode over to her, giving her a lingering kiss on the cheek.

Seraphina felt her face warm under his touch. This was so weird – but weird in a good way. She wasn't used to seeing Brandon this way. Brandon didn't seem like the sort of guy who engaged in public displays of affection, even with someone he genuinely cared about. But apparently, she was wrong because whenever they were around each other, he couldn't keep his hands off of her. And she loved that. Even though they were supposed to keep things private, try to hide their relationship from the public because anyone could recognize Brandon Thorpe, they didn't. Not when they were away from Sea Side, away from any hockey related place or event.

They headed into the diner and ordered their food. He wanted Huevos Rancheros while she ate ham and eggs with cheese on her eggs and breakfast potatoes. From there, they walked back outside and sat on a bench, facing the water crashing to the shore. It was so peaceful here. She closed her eyes and breathed in a deep breath of fresh air.

"How are you?" Brandon asked from beside her.

Seraphina slowly opened her eyes and nodded her head, giving him a small smile. "Good," she said. "And you?"

He nodded back. "Good," he said. "I got a call from my sister last night. Apparently, she wants to come out and visit in a couple of weeks." He paused. "She wants to meet you. I'll make us dinner at my place."

"You can cook?" Seraphina raised an interested brow. "I'm looking forward to it. Is she here just to visit or...?" She let her voice trail off, ripping her eyes away from the ocean and looking at Brandon's chiseled profile.

"She's here for an accounting conference," he explained. "I guess she'll be staying at a hotel up in Anaheim, but she wanted to come down and visit for a bit. She was insistent that I introduce you to her."

Seraphina felt her cheeks turn pink. "I didn't realize you had even told her about me," she murmured, picking at her food and trying to keep the smile from slipping on her face. Her stomach fluttered with butterflies at the prospect that he had talked to his family about her. She hoped they liked her – she supposed it completely depended on what Brandon actually said – but the fact that he was talking about her to them at all told her that she was important to him.

He didn't talk much, after all, and there was no way they could bring her up – at least, she thought they couldn't.

"Of course I told them about you," he told her. He paused, taking another bite of his food. Seraphina inhaled deeply, her eyes going back to the beautiful sparkling ocean. She loved it here. She loved the peacefulness the beach provided during the off-season, where only locals exercised and walked down cemented pathways. "I don't think you realize just how important you are to me."

Seraphina glanced over at him. "I feel the same way about you," she said.

Once they were finished, they threw their plastic utensils and paper plates away. Without even speaking to each other,

Brandon grabbed Seraphina's hand and they began to walk down the pathway themselves, looking at all the multi-million dollar houses. The houses in Balboa were different sizes but all were big and modern. The actual space of land was small, but they built up. Some of these houses were three stories tall with barbeques on their roofs since there was barely any room for a backyard. The majority were rented out by tourists during the summer, and they were required to pay a crazy amount of money per week just to do so. Her grandfather had mentioned wanting to invest in a couple of pieces of the property before he died but he never got around to actually doing it.

"Doesn't Drew Stefano live here?" Seraphina asked, picking her head up from his shoulder and glancing at him. "Not here, but down PCH in Balboa?"

Brandon shrugged. "I don't know," he said.

Seraphina rolled her eyes. "You really need to do a better job of getting to know your team," she said, nudging him playfully. "You're their captain. You need to lead and inspire."

"Don't I do that every night I go out there and play?" he asked.

Seraphina chuckled and rolled her eyes. "Would you ever live here?" she asked.

Brandon shrugged. "Too many people," he said. "But I wouldn't be closed off to compromising."

Seraphina smiled, leaning her head on his shoulder. "We should probably go," she murmured. "You have a team meeting. I have to see if there's anybody I can pick up for cheap before the deadline."

Brandon nodded. "Five more minutes and then we'll go," he said. "Please."

Seraphina felt her heart glow. "Five more minutes," she agreed and placed her head back on his shoulder, taking a deep breath and surrounding herself with the aroma of the ocean and Brandon Thorpe. And for those five minutes, life was perfect.

Chapter 19

SERAPHINA RETURNED to the office the next morning during the morning skate, refreshed and ready to tackle the day. She felt much better than she had the day before. After a long shower this morning and fifteen minutes of yoga, she was ready to get dressed in one of her favorite outfits – a blue blouse that brought out her eyes and a high-waisted pencil skirt with her favorite red-soled black high heels. She straightened her hair and pulled it back so half was up in a small ponytail while the other half was left down, and her bangs were swept to the side of her face.

As she walked through, passing the rink, she was tempted to stay and watch. She could see Brandon clearly, even though he was on the other side of the ice, and as usual, she was compelled to sit and watch him. It was difficult for her to take her eyes off of him.

However, she didn't want to make it obvious that they were together, especially since Bambridge made it a habit of running his mouth. Instead, she took the elevator up to the third floor, where the offices and business administration for the team were located. She said hello to their administrative secretary, a college kid who had been a Gulls' fan since she was young. She smiled in return but couldn't meet Seraphina's eye. Seraphina furrowed her brow at the odd behavior but she refused to analyze it or get offended by it. Instead, she kept her head held high as she walked down the long hallway to her office.

She opened her door and slid off her red coat, wrapping it around the back of her chair. She took a seat and turned on her computer. At that moment, her phone rang. It was the admin secretary. She furrowed her brow again. If she had just gotten to her office and the phone was already ringing, she knew it was going to be a long day.

"Phil Bambridge for you," Serena murmured.

Seraphina sighed. "Patch him through," she muttered.

There was a beat before Phil came on the line. "Seraphina Hanson," Phil said in a boisterous voice. "How the hell are you?"

"Much better than your team," she replied before she could stop herself.

There was a surprised pause and Seraphina could feel the awkwardness through the phone. She refused to allow it to affect her, however. She had done nothing wrong. Sure, the quip was somewhat underhanded but after everything he had said about her, she felt he deserved it just a little bit. She leaned back in her chair and was about to place her feet on the desk when her grandfather's voice snapped at her in her head and told her she better not dare, just as he had when she was a teenager and she would hang out here while he worked. Her eyes shifted to the blood stain in her office - formally his office - where he was murdered. They had offered to change the carpet but she refused. She liked the reminder that this used to be his, that in some kind of morbid way, he was still here.

"Yes, well." He paused and she could hear the smile back in his voice. "That's what I'm hoping to remedy, actually."

Seraphina rolled her eyes. "And what's that supposed to mean?" she asked.

"I'm calling you to propose a trade," he said. She could still hear the smirk in his voice and she had to flex her fingers to keep her digits from curling into a fist.

"A trade," she stated, her tone flat. "And why would you think I would be willing to even humor a trade with you?"

"You're a business woman, aren't you?" he asked. "At least, your little blogger who interviewed me the other night certainly seems to think so. Prove it and engage in a trade."

"I have nothing to prove here, Phil," Seraphina said. "My team is going to make playoffs, your team is not. You're the one clamoring to switch things up now. I have a team I'm satisfied with."

"Interesting choice of words," Phil said. "By team, do you mean Brandon Thorpe or do you mean the whole team? I hear that sort of thing runs in your family."

"I'm sorry, I can't hear you over the bitterness of a man who doesn't understand what no means," Seraphina said, managing to transform her temper into quick wit. "I hope you've learned by now because, once again, I'm going to have to turn you down."

"You haven't even heard my offer out," Phil pointed out. "You at least have to hear it out before you reject it. That's GM 101."

"Why don't you reserve your GM tips for someone who has less experience under your belt and for someone who actually needs it," Seraphina said. "As far as I'm concerned, my team is solid."

"You really think so?" Phil asked and she could hear the attitude in his voice with little restraint. "You don't think I won't go to the media about how you didn't even entertain my trade offer? You know that's not in good taste, Hanson."

"I don't think you get to tell me what's in good taste when Harper Crawford spanked you in front of those sports journalists," Seraphina said, leaning back in her chair. "But since this doesn't sound as though you're going to give this up anytime soon, I'd be happy to hear you out. I just want to let you know that your offer is going to be rejected. But go ahead and try."

"I want Thorpe," Bambridge said. "And I'm willing to give you Avery, Thompson, and Duke in exchange for him."

Seraphina paused. Avery was a first line winger with thirty-seven goals under his belt already. Thompson was a star defenseman who was both offensive and defensive, which meant he wasn't afraid to play up and involve himself in the play. He had thirteen goals, which was third in the league for defensemen. And Duke was a goalie with a couple of years under his belt. He was no Brandon Thorpe but he was an adequate replacement.

"I take your silence as a maybe?" Phil asked smugly.

Seraphina scowled but remembered he couldn't see her from where she was. "Absolutely not," she said. "I just can't believe you're that desperate that you're willing to give away the core of your success for my goalie."

"He is your goalie, isn't he?" Phil said. There was something in his tone, something that sent warning alarms off. "I want him to be my goalie. He's arguably the best in the league and I'm willing to give up these three players in order to acquire him. Hell, I'm even throwing in my starting goalie in return so you aren't forced to start your backup. What do you say?"

"I say-"

"Before you respond, Seraphina," he said. "I want you to think very carefully. We both know I'm overpaying for Thorpe. Yeah, he's the best but he's never even made the playoffs before. With Avery and Thompson, you'll get the offense you need to score your goals that'll get you the wins. You want a guaranteed seed spot? Give me Thorpe and you'll get it."

"There's no way I'm giving you Thorpe," she told him. "I don't care who you offer."

"Because you're in love with him," Phil stated. Before Seraphina could defend herself, Phil continued. "See, this is why

you ladies should not be in charge of making important decisions in business. You let your feelings get in the way."

"Tell me," Seraphina said. "Why do you suddenly want
Brandon? It wouldn't be your pride talking, would it?"

"Thorpe is the best goalie in the league. I would be remiss if
I didn't at least try to acquire him for my team."

Seraphina rolled her eyes. Just because he threw in one high-
frequency vocabulary word did not mean he was suddenly good
with words. She hated people who thought they were more
important than they really were.

"That's not happening," she told him.

"I think you're going to change your mind about that," Phil
said. There it was again, the smirk. The smugness.

"Well, you're —"

"Don't finish that sentence until you check your email,
Seraphina," Phil said in a sing-song voice. "Go ahead and
check. I'll wait."

"Bambridge, I don't have time for this," Seraphina said even
though she was bringing up her Outlook as she spoke. "Unlike
you, I have a team who is probably going to make playoffs and
you are just an annoying distraction. Now, can you please —"

She cut herself off when she noticed an email from Phil
with attachments. She opened it up. There was nothing written,
no text, but there were three grainy pictures of her and Brandon
swept up in a passionate kiss.

"I take your silence as you received my email," Phil said
slowly.

"What is this about?" Seraphina said through gritted teeth.
She wanted to make sure she kept her voice restrained. She
didn't want him to know that he had gotten to her in the worst
way. Her emotions had to be controlled.

"I think you know exactly what this is about," he said.
"Look, Sera, we both know what's going on between you and
Thorpe. Hell, who am I to judge? But we also know it crosses
the line of professionalism. GM's and owners cannot date their

players. If you don't give me Thorpe for that extremely generous offer I made you, I'm going to release those photos."

"This is blackmail," Seraphina said slowly. Her eyes started to prick with tears and she clenched her teeth together to keep them at bay. There was no way she was going to allow herself to cry with Phil Bambridge on the phone.

"I like to think of it as motivation to do the right thing," Phil said. "We both know you don't want these pictures leaking. And I know I want Thorpe on my team. The decision is completely up to you. You have until the twenty-eighth. You know, since March first is the trade deadline."

Seraphina hung up before he could get another word in. She didn't want to hear what else Phil had to say. She didn't want to lose her temper lest she start throwing things around her office like she was on the verge of doing. Her eyes found the blood stain underneath her desk. What once used to calm her pushed her over the edge and the tears started to fall.

She had no idea what she was going to do.

Chapter 20

ONCE MORNING SKATE WAS OVER, Brandon stopped by Seraphina's office, his bag over his shoulder, his dark brown hair dripping with water from a shower he just took. He frowned upon seeing her, probably because Seraphina's face was in her hands, her shoulders hunched forward, her elbows on her desk, wrinkling her papers. He knocked, alerting her to his presence.

She picked her head up and Brandon noticed her eyes red from crying. Immediately, Brandon tensed. He stepped into her office and shut her door before dropping the hockey bag at his feet and drawing the blinds so nobody would be able to see the two of them. He furrowed his brow, narrowing his pale green eyes as he looked at her.

"What happened?" he asked in a low voice. There was an edge to it he hadn't expected to come out of his mouth but he didn't apologize for it.

Seraphina shook her head, wiping her nose with the back of her hand and leaning back in her chair, her eyes going over to her computer screen. Brandon's heart tensed, worried she was shutting him out. She tended to do this when something happened with the team as a whole. At least, that was what he observed. It was as though she took on the burden herself and thought she needed to solve it on her own.

"It's —"

"Don't say nothing," Brandon said, interrupting her. He took a seat in front of her. Part of him wanted to reach out and take her hands within his, but something caused him to hold back, to wait. She seemed tense and he didn't want to touch her if she didn't want him to. And if he did that, he knew for certain she would keep her mouth closed and hold everything back. "Sera, I'm here for you. You can tell me anything."

Seraphina looked like she had to think about it. Brandon ignored the shot it took to his heart that her response wasn't immediate. But he kept that to himself. This wasn't about him, this was about her, and something seriously was wrong if she was this withdrawn. Seraphina was reserved, certainly, but not this much.

"Okay," she told him, "but you aren't going to like it."

Brandon's forehead wrinkled as he pushed up his brow. He tried not to make assumptions, didn't want to think this was a talk that involved them going back to the way it was, where they were friends and nothing more. He highly doubted Seraphina would do that to him. Still. He didn't like that she thought he wouldn't like it. But he wanted to give her the opportunity to at least tell him herself without jumping in and demanding answers.

She gestured at a seat across from her. "You might want to sit down," she suggested.

Brandon did as she told him, clenching his teeth together in order to keep from saying anything.

She'll tell you when she's ready, he kept chanting to himself. *She'll tell you when she's ready.*

Seraphina straightened her spine and looked at Brandon, taking care to meet his eyes with hers. She had to know it was obvious she had been crying. She probably hated the fact that she couldn't wipe away the evidence. Not that she liked to hide herself from him, per se, but he knew she didn't like to appear vulnerable.

"Phil Bambridge requested a trade," she said, each word sharp and enunciated. "He wants you in exchange for three of his core players."

Brandon furrowed his brow once more. "Who?" he asked.

"I don't think that's relevant," Seraphina told him. "I'm not going to do it."

"Then why have you been crying?" Brandon could hear his heart thump through his mind, like an echo reminding him that just because Seraphina was the love of his life didn't mean she also wasn't a business woman.

Seraphina pressed her lips together and turned to her computer. Brandon almost snapped at her to focus on what was going on now instead of hiding away behind her computer. However, when she stopped typing, she locked eyes with him and nodded her head, silently beckoning him to come over and look at her monitor.

Brandon stood up and walked around her desk. She pointed to three pictures on the screen and immediately, Brandon recognized him and Seraphina wrapped up in each other in a passionate kiss. He recognized that kiss. It was their first kiss, one he initiated because she had pushed him to the point where he couldn't help but kiss her, not with what she was saying. Plus, he wanted to kiss her and needed a reason to. He knew how she felt about dating players and how it would make her look to the public, but in that moment, he couldn't be bothered to care.

He had to kiss her. So he did. And the best part was when she kissed him back.

To be honest, Brandon hadn't even realized someone had been taking pictures. He had forgotten that other people were even there in the first place. All he cared about was that moment with her in his arms and his lips on hers. She had felt perfect, he didn't want to let her go. Hell, he wasn't planning on it until Bambridge made his presence known.

In a way, Brandon was glad that Bambridge had seen them. He had never been the guy to believe in marking territory, so to speak, but at least Bambridge would know Seraphina belonged to him, and if anything happened to her while she was with Bambridge, Brandon had no problem taking care of it.

Except something had happened and Brandon had done nothing. And now, Bambridge was using it to his advantage.

"What the hell is this?" Brandon asked, tilting his head to look at Seraphina.

"He has pictures of us," Seraphina said, glancing over at him and raising a brow. "I don't know how he got them. I don't know if he saw what was going on and then took a couple of pictures or if someone else took pictures and he managed to get his hands on them. I guess in the end, it doesn't really matter." She snorted and rolled her eyes at the last sentence that came out of her mouth. It was too ridiculous, the situation too tense, and Seraphina couldn't help but laugh awkwardly.

Brandon raised his brow at her behavior but didn't comment, which was probably a good thing.

"So he's threatening to release these photos publicly unless you go through with the trade?" Brandon guessed, standing up straight and crossing his arms over his chest.

"Pretty much," she said.

Brandon clenched his jaw. Seraphina could feel his fury rolling off of him in hard, choppy waves. It was the kind of anger someone could drown in if they were pulled tightly into his orbit.

"So," he said slowly, through gritted teeth, "what are we going to do?"

"I'm not going to go through with the trade, obviously," Seraphina told him, picking her eyes up so she could lock eyes with him. She hoped he knew that, that she didn't have to actually say that, but she wanted to anyway, just to make sure he really understood.

"When do you have until?" Brandon asked.

"The twenty-eighth."

Seraphina continued to watch Brandon with wide eyes, wondering what he was thinking about why he was so mad. Yes, of course, the situation was extremely frustrating. Seraphina had spent the past fifteen minutes crying over it. But she didn't want Brandon to think the situation was hopeless, that nothing could be done.

"What are you going to do about this?" he finally asked. His words were clipped, as though he was trying to figure out what should be done but he also recognized that this was her problem and she needed to make a decision about this as well.

"I..." Seraphina pressed her lips together. Perhaps she should have been researching her options rather than crying about the predicament she was in. She clenched her jaw and internally shook her head at herself. She couldn't believe she had been so selfish. So helpless. Her grandfather raised her better than that. *Don't mope. Solve the problem the right way.* "Honestly, I don't know. I just know what I'm not going to do."

Brandon nodded once, quick jabs of movement. "We need to figure this out, Sera," he told her. "The twenty-eighth is only a couple of days away. He could release those photos at any second and –"

"I know," she snapped. "Don't you think I know this? I don't know what I should do, Brandon. If you have any suggestions, please let me know."

He ran his hand through his hair and shook his head. "Hell if I know," he said. "Your grandfather's received offers for me before but he never took them. As far as I know, he never even considered them."

"Yes," Seraphina said slowly. "The difference being that my grandfather isn't around and if he was, I highly doubt he'd be getting blackmailed right now." She pressed her lips together. "Brandon, what the hell should I do? Should I resign? I could give the team to Kat, but she's with Negan and..." She groaned, shaking her head.

"Have you spoken to your lawyer?" Brandon asked. Seraphina could tell he was trying to keep his own patience, but she didn't know if it was due to her erratic behavior or because of the situation in general. "Maybe she'll be able to help you figure this whole thing out. That's why you have her on your payroll, right? Talk to her and figure it out." He placed his hand on Seraphina's shoulder, giving it a squeeze. "I'm here for you."

Seraphina forced a smile and placed her hand over his. "Thanks," she said. "How are you?"

"Honestly, I'd like to fly to Vegas and beat the shit out of Bambridge," Brandon said, "but I don't think that's the healthiest response to what's going on." He looked down at her, his pale green eyes brimming with grass-green frustration. "I wish I could do more for you, Sera. I feel like I can't help you at all and I'm pissed because it's my fault we're in this situation in the first place."

Seraphina furrowed her brow, cocking her head so she could look up at him with a questioning stare. "What do you mean, your fault?" she asked.

"*I* kissed *you*," he reminded her. "I was sick and tired of waiting for you –"

"For me!" Seraphina exclaimed. "I've been waiting for you to make your move. I just, I've been with a few guys that I'd pursued. I wanted to know I was worth the chase, that someone would go out of their way to try and be with me."

"And when I did, you ran," Brandon pointed out.

"I ran," Seraphina agreed. "I had no idea what I was doing, what I was going to do. But that still doesn't make the kiss your fault. I need to talk to my lawyer." She met Brandon's eyes, her tone firm. "We need to figure this out because I'm not going to let Bambridge try and take you from me. From this team."

"What happens when we run out of options, Sera?" Brandon asked. There was an edge to his voice, a sound that wasn't familiar to Seraphina's ears. She didn't like it, truth be told. It was negative and angry and frustrated all at one time.

"What happens when your lawyer comes back to us and tells us that we're screwed. I would rather you trade me than give the uncles your team."

"We don't even know if that's what it's going to come down to," Seraphina said. "Please. Don't talk like this."

"What do you expect, Sera?" he asked. He wasn't yelling, exactly, but his words were pointed and sharp. "You were right about everything. Our first kiss and it's being used to blackmail you into either admitting you love me or getting rid of me."

Before Brandon could continue, Seraphina reached up and pulled his head down so she could lock lips with him. He was tense under her touch but after a moment, relaxed into it and allowed her to kiss him.

"I'm sorry," he said, taking a step back. "I can't think about anything else. Not until we figure this out."

"Brandon –"

"I can't lose you, Sera," he told her. "I love you. And I have you. You aren't the type of girl I can just let go of."

Before she could stop him, Brandon left, all but slamming her office door behind him.

Chapter 21

SERAPHINA WAS in the Sea Side gym when Katella found her. Seraphina was in workout clothes – shorts that just covered her backside and a tank top that clutched her curves and kept everything in place. Her hair was thrown up into a ponytail and her earphones were in her ears. She was running; even though she absolutely detested it, but she needed a healthy way to get the frustration out of her system. And this seemed like the most logical choice. Interestingly enough, it seemed to be working.

She had been here for the past couple of hours, going between running and walking and then back to running. She started out cycling but needed to stretch her legs, needed to move her entire body and pretend she was actually getting somewhere. Because she certainly wasn't getting anywhere with her personal and professional life.

"Sera."

Seraphina glanced to her right and found her sister in a light blue Gulls shirt and white jeans. She had no idea how Katella could look so pretty without putting much effort into her appearance. Even now, the only makeup she had on was lip gloss and mascara.

Seraphina nodded at her sister but made no move to get off the treadmill. Katella rolled her eyes and reached over to turn the treadmill off. Seraphina furrowed her brow and shot Katella a look.

"Can I help you with something?" she asked as the treadmill came to a stop.

"Yeah, you can tell me what the heck is going on Sera," Katella said. "You've been incredibly withdrawn all day. I saw Brandon stomp out of your office and he looked pissed. I don't even think you've had lunch yet, and you've been running for who knows how long. I'm allowed to be concerned about my baby sister. I'm allowed to check on you."

Seraphina looked like she wanted to respond. She wanted to snap back, but she couldn't. She was exhausted and Katella was right. Seraphina was acting off, Brandon was pissed for good reason, and Seraphina was… exhausted.

"What's going on, Sera?" Katella asked. "Did you and Brandon get into a fight?"

"What?" Seraphina furrowed her brow and shook her head. "No. No, of course not."

"Then why did he stomp out of your office, completely pissed off?" Katella asked, placing her hands on her hips.

Seraphina looked away. "Because Phil Bambridge is black-mailing me," she said in a low voice. "And he's using Brandon to do it."

Katella's eyes went wide and she took a step back. "How's he going to do that?" she asked in a voice just above a whisper even though there was no one else in the gym.

Seraphina clenched her jaw and looked away. She hadn't told Katella about the moment she had shared with Brandon in the lobby of the Vegas hotel while she was waiting for Phil Bambridge. She hadn't told anyone about that kiss. Now, Phil was ready to tell everyone, to reveal something that needed to be kept secret.

"Brandon and I kissed in the lobby," Seraphina told Katella.

"It just happened. We were arguing and he just kissed me and I let him. I even kissed him back. But Phil caught us. Apparently, he whipped out his cell phone and took three shitty pictures of me and Brandon while we were kissing before he let us know that he was even there." Seraphina furrowed her brow and shook her head. "I never should have…" She couldn't even finish that sentence. If she finished that sentence, that meant that she would have to regret the kiss. And despite the predicament she and Brandon were in at this moment, there was absolutely no way she could ever regret that kiss. "I got swept away, Kat. I didn't even realize he was there. Hell, I completely forgot that anybody else was there. That's how distracted I was. I feel like such an idiot."

Katella reached out and gently squeezed her sister's shoulder. "Don't feel like an idiot," she said. "We all get swept away in kisses, especially if they're from our true loves."

Seraphina raised an eyebrow at her sister. Katella rolled her eyes.

"Look," she said, "I know it sounds corny, okay? Trust me. Negan and I have only been dating for six weeks but I already know that he's the one I'm going to settle down with, the one I'm going to have kids with. I can't explain how I know, I just do. So when you tell me Brandon kissed you and you forgot about everything and everyone else, I believe you. You don't have to explain it. What I need you to explain is why Phil Bambridge is blackmailing you. Are the pictures definitively you and Brandon? Can you make the argument that there's nothing conclusive about them?"

Seraphina shrugged. "I can show you them so you can see them for yourself," she offered. "I feel as though I'm too close to it to see things from the outside. I know what I wore and I know Brandon like the back of my hand. Phil saw us so he definitely knows that's us. Brandon did say something about how no one for sure knows it one way or the other but I'm not sure I want to take that risk. It isn't just about me, you know? It's about

Brandon and the team and ugh." She gripped her forehead before dropping her hand. "I can't believe I got into this mess. Not that I regret the kiss, but…"

"Well, let's not stress right this second," Katella suggested. "You know who you should talk to before you even get the lawyers involved? Talk to Drew Stefano. He might know laws and what the best way to handle this would be."

Seraphina nodded. "I'll call him right now," she said. "After I shower, I mean."

"Good idea," Katella said, wrinkling her nose playfully. "You smell."

Seraphina smiled despite herself. Count on Katella to say the most ridiculous things to get a smile out of her.

<hr>

DREW STEFANO WAS good looking and reserved. He was actually very similar to Brandon in personality but with a touch of awkwardness about him, like he knew his position on the ice, but when he was participating in fan events, he wasn't sure how to act or how to handle himself.

His team gave him shit because there was one fan he seemed to stare at a lot, even though he had a serious girlfriend who acted and did an online talk show for a cable network. From what Seraphina knew, she had blonde hair and was very pretty, but not as put-together as women in the acting world where makeup covered their whole face and they went to a salon before a game.

"Hey," Seraphina said with a warm smile.

To say Drew Stefano looked uncomfortable would be an understatement. He kept shifting in his seat, almost as though he was expecting the other foot to drop.

"So, I'm not trading you," Seraphina told him. "You don't have to worry about that." Drew's shoulders sagged forward and a sigh of relief came out of his mouth. "Sorry, I hadn't even thought that it would totally seem like I was having a meeting with you to tell you that you were being traded. My bad. But we want to hang on to you for as long as we can. You're an integral part of our team, Drew."

"So what do you need?" Drew asked. The question came out insistent and perhaps a little sharp but that was probably because he was still getting over the fact that he wasn't being traded like he originally assumed.

"You majored in criminology, right?" At Drew's nod, Seraphina continued. "Okay. I need your help in whatever way you can help me. I'm going to talk to you about some sensitive information that I'd like you to keep between you and me. Can you do that?"

Drew quirked a brow, somewhat confused and perhaps a tad intrigued. However, he nodded his head. Seraphina smiled and told him everything – not that she and Brandon were serious about each other but they kissed, Bambridge had pictures, and now he was blackmailing her into a trade that would see the team lose Thorpe.

"So I need to know what to do that doesn't have me lose Thorpe, put a target on his back or mine, and how to get Phil Bambridge from releasing the photos," Seraphina concluded, almost breathless. "I know that's a lot of information, most you didn't particularly care about. But I trust you and I'd love to get any advice you can give me."

"Honestly, I would talk to your lawyer about this," Drew said. "Just to understand what your legal responsibilities are, what you can and can't do based on what the NHL expects, and how to combat this. However, you asked for my advice, so I'm going to give it to you: in my opinion – and this is in no way actual legal advice – you should take away Bambridge's power."

Seraphina furrowed her brows and gave Drew a long look. "And how should I go about doing that?" she asked. "He has the pictures, not me."

"I know," Drew said with a nod. "But you don't need the

pictures. Come out head on against him and it takes away all of his power."

"So," Seraphina said slowly, shifting her eyes to Drew before looking down at her planner, "you want me to actually admit Brandon and I kissed?"

Drew shook his head. "It does not have to be as obvious as that," he said. "All you need to do is come out, tell everyone he's blackmailing you. You don't have to get into the specifics. It could be something generic and imply that he's acting on sexist assumptions. It's completely your call."

"By doing this, what happens?" Seraphina asked, pushing her brows together. "I apologize for my ignorance but what does this help me gain?"

"Like I said," Drew said with a small grin, "it takes away his power. Let's say you call a press conference and say Bambridge is blackmailing me because he is saying I won't take his trade due to the fact that he believes Thorpe and I are having an affair. By talking about it before he does, you control what gets released and what doesn't. Sure, they may question Bambridge and sure, he may release the photos just to spite you. But he's making a power move and if he has no power, he has no move."

"He has no move," Seraphina murmured to herself, her eyes shining. She stood and stuck out her hand. "Thank you very much for this incredibly informative discussion, Drew. You have no idea how helpful this was to me. Thank you."

Drew stood and shook her hand. He seemed unsure, like he didn't really think it was already over. "Yeah, no worries," he said.

When he left, Seraphina picked up her office phone and dialed Brandon's number. He picked up on second ring. "Brandon?" she asked after he greeted her with a hello. "How are you?"

"Still frustrated," was his response. "I haven't thought of a way out of this mess."

"I think I have an idea," she said. "I talked to Drew and I'm going to set up an emergency meeting with my lawyer later today if possible, but Drew gave me an idea. I wanted to talk about it with you before I make any decisions because this does involve you. Do you have the time?"

"Yeah, of course," he said. He paused and Seraphina could hear him sigh through his nose. "I'm sorry about earlier. I hate not being able to do anything and I just –"

"Hey, it's okay," Seraphina said quickly. "There's no need to apologize."

"Listen, we're still on for tomorrow night, right?" Brandon asked, almost tentatively. "With my sister?"

Seraphina's brow pushed. She had completely forgotten about dinner with Cameron Thorpe. She had been too distracted by what was going on that she hadn't even remembered to be stressed at the fact that she was meeting Brandon's sister or elated that they were at this step in their new relationship.

"Of course," she managed to say.

"Are you sure?" he asked. "You hesitated."

She rolled her eyes.

"And you rolled your eyes."

"Everything will be fine, Brandon," she said, trying to hide her attitude. Damn him for knowing her too well. "I will be at your place tomorrow night. I'm really looking forward to meeting Cameron. Okay, got to go, love you!"

And she hung up before she could hear his laughter.

Chapter 22

SERAPHINA ARRIVED at Brandon's place just after six o'clock in the evening. The sun was already down, the night black, save for the half-moon that glowed almost supernaturally. That would change in the next couple of weeks, thanks to Daylight Savings Time. Seraphina wasn't looking forward to losing an hour of sleep but she was excited about the sun staying out until seven or eight o'clock at night.

Her heart fluttered in her chest, which was ridiculous since they had already slept together, had already confessed their love for each other. They were already serious about each other; there shouldn't be any logical reason for her to be nervous. Save for the fact that this was the first time Seraphina had ever been to Brandon's place before and she didn't know what to expect.

Oh, and his sister was visiting. Again. And the last time his sister was here, Seraphina hadn't realized that was his sister and thought she was some woman who had a thing for Brandon Thorpe and might have unwittingly shot her a couple of dirty looks.

She hesitated, sitting in her car and looking at the one-story house. It was a relatively modest house in the Westcliffe neighborhood. She smiled at how quiet it was here. It was the perfect place for him. This neighborhood was filled with retirees. Unless they were Gulls' fans, they would have no idea who he was.

This was the absolute worst time for her to be meeting one of the most important people in Brandon's life. Seraphina's head was everywhere. She was worried about those photos leaking, she was worried about the possibility of giving Brandon up to Vegas, she was worried about him being forced to retire just so they wouldn't get in trouble. No matter what option she chose, Phil Bambridge won. And that was the worst thing about the whole situation – the fact that there was a good chance Seraphina wouldn't be able to think about something where Bambridge didn't win. Where the photos weren't released, where Brandon didn't go to Vegas, and where he didn't have to quit the playoffs right before the end of the season.

Don't focus on that right now, a voice in her head pointed out. *This is a little more important than that.*

Seraphina got out of the car and grabbed a box of assorted chocolates. She had no idea what to get her and she thought flowers or a Visa gift card would be too tacky. Brandon had mentioned she liked chocolate so this was the best Seraphina could come up with. She walked up to the door and knocked with the back of her hand, shifting her weight from foot to foot.

At that moment, the door opened and a beautiful blonde woman beamed down at Seraphina. She had the same pale green eyes Brandon had, the same sharp jaw, the same cheekbones. The only difference, really, was the hair color. And the fact that Cameron seemed to smile way more than her younger brother.

"Hi," Cameron said, reaching out her hand. "I'm Cameron. Brandon has told me so much about you!"

"Hi," Seraphina said, her lips curling up as she shifted her eyes in order to look for Brandon.

Brandon popped up behind his sister and shrugged, almost

as if to say, *She insisted on answering the door and I'm powerless to stop her from doing anything.*

Seraphina refrained from rolling her eyes and held out her gift. "This is for you," she said. "Brandon wouldn't really give me many details about what you like and what you don't so I had to make do with what I know about girls and how much they love chocolate."

Cameron's eyes widened and a smile slid onto her face. "I *love* chocolate," she said. "Especially the expensive kind."

"Sera, won't you come in?" Brandon said, finally deciding now would be the perfect time to invite his girlfriend inside his home. "Unless you want her to eat outside, Cam."

Cameron rolled her eyes. "Okay, Smartass," she said, but she gave Seraphina a smile and stepped aside so Seraphina could walk into the house without any obstruction.

Brandon walked over and gave Seraphina a peck on the cheek, taking her hands in his. He leaned down to her ear and whispered, "I apologize in advance for anything that comes out of her mouth."

"So it is true," Cameron said, setting the box down on the marble island in the middle of the kitchen. "My baby brother has finally found himself a serious girlfriend. When are you going to bring her home? I'm sure Mom would love to meet her. She's constantly going on and on about grandchildren and we both know I'm not going to give her any." She looked back at Seraphina. "I actually prefer girls."

"Oh." Seraphina nodded once. "Good for you. When I was going through a breakup in high school, I wanted to be a lesbian because women are so much easier to be around and understand than men are."

"Sometimes," Cameron said.

"You know we just started dating, right?" Brandon asked his sister, quirking a brow. "You're talking about us like –"

"Like what?" Cameron interrupted. "Like you haven't been talking about her for the last year and a half? Hmm, okay. So you aren't serious? She could just go out and date somebody else, then?"

Brandon shot his sister a dark look and she laughed. "That's what I thought," she said. "See, Brandon? You are serious about her. There's nothing wrong with that at all. I'm glad, actually. If anyone deserves to be in a serious relationship, it's you."

Brandon rolled his eyes. "Can we get this dinner over with?" he asked, walking back into the kitchen. Seraphina's eyes found his butt-clad in form-fitting sweatpants without even trying. Immediately, her eyes snapped away. There was no way she wanted Cameron to catch her staring at her brother's butt, even if it was an amazing butt. "The food is going to get cold."

"Well, we can't have that," Cameron said, and looped her arm through Brandon's. "Come sit by me. I want to know everything about you."

Seraphina felt her face turn red but she followed Cameron over to the far side of the table and took a seat next to her. From there, Cameron asked her everything she possibly could to learn about Seraphina. Seraphina, in turn, was as honest as she could be: she had no idea what she was doing when she had inherited the team but she learned as much as she could, as fast as she could. She didn't want to sell the team because she wanted to keep her grandfather's legacy alive. When Brandon was accused of killing her grandfather, Seraphina had no idea why she thought Brandon was innocent other than a gut feeling.

"You must have a big pair of balls to have believed in my brother when no one else did," Cameron murmured, taking a long sip of red wine. "Especially when it would have been easier to just support the police no matter what, as a new owner and manager, of course."

Seraphina shrugged. "Yeah, well," she said. "My team is my priority. Not what anyone thinks of me."

"Clearly," Cameron muttered. "The media likes to talk a lot of shit about you that has nothing to do with hockey."

Seraphina snorted. "Don't I know it," she said.

"So I take it you and Brandon aren't going to be public anytime soon?" Cameron asked, though there was no judgment in her tone. She looked between Seraphina and Brandon, who sat directly across from Seraphina.

"I support whatever decision she makes," Brandon said, looking over at Seraphina. "As long as I get to be with her, I'm willing to do whatever it takes."

Cameron rolled her eyes. "I never expected you to be such a romantic," she said to Brandon. "Really. I think a lot of the girls you were with before would have hung on to you if they had known you even had the ability to talk like this."

Brandon shrugged. "I don't particularly care about them," he replied.

"Typical male," she said. "See, this is why I like girls."

The three ate in friendly company, with Cameron telling long stories about Brandon as a child. This amused Seraphina to no end; it was eye-opening and explained a lot about how quiet and reserved he was, even as a captain.

"But here's what I don't get," Cameron said, looking between the couple. "How did someone as quiet as you get to be team captain?"

Seraphina chuckled and Brandon shrugged. "It was after out last home game my third season with the team," Brandon said. "Ken was there and he gave a little speech about how he was proud of us but that he expected us to work hard in the off-season to come back strong. He really believed with could make playoffs if every piece fit together just right, and he thought that as long as we put in the work, we would be rewarded. And then, in front of the team, after Sammy Sanders announced his retirement, he asked the team to vote. Everyone said yes, so next year, I got the C."

Seraphina gave her boyfriend a grin. "I remember that," she said. "My grandfather talked to me before the game. I think I was still in high school. He wanted to know if I thought you deserved to be captain. He said the guys weren't too friendly with you because you can be standoffish."

"Not a lie," Cameron murmured.

"I told my grandfather that while it does matter what the team thinks of you as a player, it doesn't really matter what they think of you as a person," Seraphina continued. "If they follow you regardless of how quiet you are and if you come to the ice every day with passion for the sport and effort, then, of course, you deserve the C. But the team should vote on it because it's a team thing, not a Grandpa thing."

Brandon gave her a long look, a look that sent shivers down her spine and settle in her pelvis. A look that caused her tummy to erupt with butterflies and fireworks at the same time.

"Okay," Cameron said, standing up. "Well, I'm going to go."

"No, there's no need –" Brandon said as Seraphina asked, "Are you sure?"

"Look," Cameron said, staring between the two. "When you guys are making goo-goo eyes across the table at each other, that's my cue to get the hell out. I really don't need to see that, even though it's a nice change of pace."

Brandon and Seraphina stood and Brandon pulled Cameron into a tight hug. "Thanks for coming, Cam," he murmured.

"Of course, thanks for having me." Cameron broke from her brother and pulled Seraphina into a tight hug. "You lucked out with this one, Brandon. Don't fuck it up." Her eyes found Seraphina's. "Be patient with my brother. Please. He means well, I promise. When he gets frustrated, he withdraws into himself and he needs someone who can bring himself out – if that makes any sense."

Seraphina nodded. "It does," she said. "It was lovely meeting you."

"Also," Cameron said as they walked her to the door, "you're lucky to have my brother. I hope you know that." Seraphina paused and gave Cameron a gentle smile. "I know you're risking a lot, being with him. But he's risking a lot by being with you, too."

Seraphina nodded. "You're right," she acknowledged. "But I know I'm lucky to even breathe the same air he does."

Cameron scrunched her nose. "I can't deal with such saps," she said, opening the door. "Okay, I'm out. Thanks again!"

Chapter 23

"SO?" Brandon asked, cocking his head to the side.

"So… what?" Seraphina asked, scrunching her brows from her seat on the couch. She was on her second glass of wine and was leaning against the pillows behind her, her head slightly fuzzy. She felt extremely relaxed.

Brandon chuckled. "My sister," he said, coming to sit next to her and gently taking the glass of wine from her hand. "What did you think of my sister?"

"She's wonderful," Seraphina said as though it was the most obvious thing in the world. "The real question is what she thought of me."

"Honestly?" Brandon asked. "She's just happy I've started dating again. The fact that you're educated and beautiful and successful is just the cherry on top."

Seraphina felt herself grin. "Well," she said. "I really liked her. I'm honored that she wanted to meet me. Even though she grilled me like a drill sergeant."

"That's her being protective," he told her. He coiled his arm around her shoulders and pulled her to him so her head hit his chest. "I'm glad you're with me."

"I'm glad you're with me," she replied. There was a pause, and then, "what are we going to do?" Seraphina hadn't meant to ask that question. This moment wasn't about stress or worry. This was about relaxing with red wine and enjoying each other's company. But she couldn't help it. She wanted to come up with a plan. She wanted to finish this *now* so she could go back to worrying about playoffs.

"We could go to the police," he suggested.

"I just don't want the police involved," Seraphina said. "I want to be able to handle this on my own."

"Seraphina, it's okay if you can't," Brandon told her. "That's what I'm here for. That's what Katella is here for. Your team. Your staff. They all want to be here for you. When you take this on your own, you won't win. But if you ask for help, you'll get it. I'm sure someone will think of something."

"I thought you wanted to keep this kind of close to the chest," Seraphina murmured, closing her eyes so she could hear the beating of Brandon's heart. "You told the whole team it was no one's business."

"Well maybe I was wrong," Brandon said, shrugging one shoulder. "I can admit that I was being protective over you and that meant leaving the team in the dark. But maybe it would be better if they knew. It would show you trusted them."

Seraphina nodded. "I agree," she said. "I also want to get Harper to write a follow-up article to the one she put out after interviewing Bambridge."

He nodded his head. "Basically attack this before he even has a chance to make good on his threat?" he asked.

Seraphina nodded her head. "Do you think it would be low if I did the same to him?" she asked, turning to look at him once again. She had been toying with the idea ever since she got off the phone with him. One of her good friends from high school was a private investigator and Seraphina would have no problem paying her if she needed to. There had to be some kind of dirt on him, something just as bad as making out with a player and getting grainy snapshots. But there was something inside of Seraphina that told her not to do that, that stooping to his level made her just like him, even if he deserved it.

"What do you mean?" Brandon asked, cocking his head to the side. His hand found hers and he turned it over so he could trace little patterns on the inside of her wrist. "Blackmail him?"

Seraphina nodded but her heart wasn't in it. She already knew the answer… unless Brandon could think of a good reason to do it. Maybe she shouldn't completely write it off.

"Of course not, Sera," he told her, letting his fingers linger on the skin of her arm. "You're better than that."

"I know," she told him with a nod. He leaned forward, still keeping his grip on her, as he set the glass of wine on the table. "I know. I just… I want to protect this team and you and myself and… I don't know what I'm doing anymore. This whole thing has completely thrown me off and made me doubt myself and all of my decisions."

Brandon pressed his lips together and nodded. He was silent for a long moment, but Seraphina didn't mind. She knew he was thinking of the right thing to say. Which she could appreciate, considering she would rather have him be silent rather than have him say the wrong thing.

"I think you should consider taking Drew Stefano's advice," he said. "I know it's not exactly what you want but there might be some pros to taking this head-on, admitting fault, and letting the chips fall where they may."

"Admitting fault would mean acknowledging the kiss was wrong," Seraphina said, her eyes flaring gold.

"The kiss was not wrong," Brandon said, his voice sharp. He softened the look on his face and he pressed his lips together. "I know that and you know that. As people, we didn't do anything wrong. But we're not just people. I'm a Gulls player and you're my boss. In that sense, we acted based on our emotions and not in a way that was best for the team." He leaned his forehead towards hers until it rested on hers. "No matter what you do decide to do, Sera, I support you."

She couldn't stop herself from kissing him if she tried.

The kiss turned heated and he pulled her into his lap, cupping her cheek and tilting her head back so he had better access to explore her mouth. He tasted like wine and she felt herself get lightheaded because he was so damn good at kissing and he tasted fucking delicious.

He tugged at the hemline of her shirt, and without breaking the kiss, she raised her arms so he could take her shirt off and throw it on the floor. His hands immediately went to her bra-covered breasts, squeezing them and causing her to gasp. Her fingers found the back of his head and she ran her fingers through his hair, tugging gently at the roots and making him grunt with approval.

His hands wrapped around her back and skillfully managed to unhook the back of her bra and slid it off of her chest. His mouth immediately went to take a nipple between his lips and she pressed him against her chest tightly.

"Oh, yes, please," she begged, feeling her core get moist.

He grabbed hold of her hips and placed her on her back so he was on top of her. Her legs instinctively hooked around his waist and her hands clamored at his shirt before tugging it off of him and throwing it somewhere. Her hands immediately found his waist, his stomach, his abdomen.

"You're so beautiful," she mumbled into his mouth, in between kissing him. "So goddamn beautiful."

His hands found her jeans and he unbuttoned them before breaking free from her so he could tug them off of her. He pulled off her boy shorts slowly, as though the lacy material was flimsy and needed to be treated with great care. The entire time he was taking off his clothes, he did not remove his eyes from hers. The look was deep and intense and it somehow had the power to cause her lips to soak with desire.

Once she was completely naked, he stood and pulled off the

rest of his clothes. Seraphina's eyes immediately went to his cock and she felt her mouth water, her body tingling with anticipation. It twitched under her gaze and she leaned forward so she put the tip in her mouth. Brandon's eyes rolled to the back of his head and he nearly lost his balance as he let out a groan. This only encouraged Seraphina and she took him deeper into her mouth, coating him in her saliva.

"Oh, fuck," he cried out, placing his right hand in her hair. He didn't guide her to take more of him but his grip was tight and insistent.

She grabbed his cock with her free hand and began to gently stroke his length in time with her mouth's ministrations. His jaw went slack and his grip on her tightened. She honestly believed that if he hadn't been holding onto her, his knees would have given out and he would have collapsed.

"You have to stop," he finally managed to get out. "I'm going to come in your mouth, and as much as I want that, I'd love to come in you much more."

Without warning, he climbed on top of her and nudged her legs apart with his knee. He pushed himself inside of her before Seraphina could catch her breath and she let out a cry as he filled her up entirely.

This wasn't romantic in the slightest. His thrusting was hard and fast, and the way he held her down let him feel like he was in complete control. There was absolutely nothing she could do to move, to push him off, but there was no desire in her to even do so. She loved when he was on top of her, loved when he was inside of her.

She managed to slide her hand in between their bodies and allowed her fingers to dance across her exposed clit. There was no way she was going to come with his thrusting this way without some help.

When he saw her touching herself, he stopped for only a beat before taking her legs and putting them over his shoulders. He went slower but deeper and she shifted with slight discomfort mixed with a swarm of pleasure. She didn't stop touching herself. From this position, Brandon could lean forward and caress her nipples while he thrust inside of her.

And then, Seraphina felt her insides tingle and her breathing got heavier.

"That's right, Sera," Brandon murmured, looking down at her with dark, half-hooded eyes. "Come for me. Come all over my cock."

And she obeyed without even questioning him. How did he have such power over her? And he didn't even have to try. She just followed him blindly like she was in a cult and he was her leader.

He groaned as he felt her walls tighten against his cock, soaking him with her juices. And then she felt his own change in demeanor, his intake of breath and then a growl as he released himself into her.

When he finished, he stayed inside of her for as long as he could. They were silent and sleep and Seraphina was certain she could fall asleep underneath him on his couch and still be comfortable.

"You ready for tomorrow?" Brandon murmured against her shoulder.

"I'm not worried about that now," she told him, keeping her eyes shut. "You're with me now. And that's all I care about."

Chapter 24

HARPER WALKED into Seraphina's office exactly on time. Seraphina liked how punctual Harper was, how she could count on the blogger to do exactly what was asked of her without question. She wore a simple black v-neck shirt and light blue skinny jeans. Her bangs were pinned back from her face so she could give Seraphina and Brandon her full attention.

"Oh," she said when she saw Brandon, standing next to Seraphina behind her desk. It was almost as though he were some kind of bodyguard. Seraphina hoped she wasn't intimidated. Brandon insisted on being here, and since this involved him, she thought he had a right to be here. Plus, she would be lying if she said she didn't want him here. His presence always seemed to soothe her and she felt as though she could do anything when he was by her side. "I didn't realize... Do you want me to come back? I can come back."

Seraphina smiled. "You aren't interrupting anything, Harper," Seraphina insisted. "Brandon and I wanted to talk to you about your next article."

"Oh?" Harper looked between the two, interest written on her face.

"Your last one was so good on the hypocrisies of gender expectation in the business of hockey," Seraphina said. "I wanted you to do a follow-up with specific examples."

Harper's brows shot straight up in the sky. "Okay," she said with a small grin. "Sounds good."

"You aren't going to be making any friends with this article," Brandon pointed out. Seraphina pressed her lips together to keep an amused smile from breaking out onto her face. He always sounded so serious about everything, so stoic and morose.

"I didn't with my last one," Harper said. "Although that one hit Yahoo and Puck Daddy asked me to be a correspondent, which I turned down. I'm very happy where I am."

Seraphina's brows pressed up. "I didn't know that," she said.

Harper shrugged. "It's not a big deal," she said.

"Yes, it is," Seraphina said, reaching for the phone. "Hang on one second." She typed in a four-digit extension. Finance picked up on first ring. "Hi Lyla, this is Sera. Can you add a five thousand dollar increase to Harper's salary, please? I'll send the formal request over the intranet now but I wanted you to get it on the books for next check. Thanks."

Harper's eyes were wide when Seraphina hung up the phone and gave her a friendly smile. "Now that that's taken care of," she said, "Brandon called a team meeting in an hour and I want you to be there. I'm going to go into detail about what happened. Everything that's happening. I'm tired of hiding. I'm tired of doing what I think is best for my grandfather's team and start doing what's best for mine. We're going to be honest but that doesn't mean we're going to reveal everything. My relationship with Brandon is still private but I want to address Phil Bambridge and what he's doing."

There was a slow smile that crawled onto Harper's face and her forest green eyes lit up with delight. "Okay," she said with a nod. "I'm totally down."

"Are you sure?" Seraphina asked, her face serious. "I'm glad you're enthusiastic, Harper, but I want you to know that you're going to be a target, too. Bambridge has already talked shit about you to the press and even though he's a new GM trying to find his way, he has a lot of friends in high places."

Harper shrugged. "I don't care about that, Sera," she said. "What he's doing isn't right and it's totally sexist. I never even thought about owning a team one day or even managing an actual NHL club. But you're doing it. You give other little girls who might actually want to do the same thing hope. And that's important. And girls shouldn't be afraid to come to positions of power with fear because some man is threatened by her and wants to take her down using gender-associated scare tactics. I'm behind you one hundred percent, Sera. No matter what happens, I've got your back."

Seraphina felt her eyes tear up. She had been crying a lot lately, and quite frankly, she was annoyed with herself.

"Now, you might want to talk to Zach about this before you agree to anything," Seraphina told Harper, trying to keep the shakiness out of her voice. "You're going to put yourself out on the line by doing this and I want you to realize that other players may target Zachary Ryan by using you to try and goad him into a fight. I have an idea of how Zach might react but some players want their women to act a certain way so they can't be used against the players."

Harper snorted. "Zach definitely doesn't care how I act," she said. "Granted, maybe I should try a little harder when I show up at his games in yoga pants and his jersey but he seems to think I'm beautiful no matter what. He won't be ashamed of me, he'd be proud. But I'll talk to him even though I know he's going to tell me to do what I think is right. And writing this article is what's right."

Seraphina felt her lips curl up. "Okay," she said. "The meeting with the team is in an hour. I'm going to call a press conference for tomorrow, which just so happens to be my deadline, and let everyone know what I've decided. I'll see you in the locker room?"

Harper nodded. "Absolutely," she said with a grin.

Seraphina nodded. Once Harper was gone, she glanced at Brandon. "We're doing the right thing, right?" she asked.

He clutched her shoulder with his hand and gave it a squeeze as he kissed the top of her head. "Absolutely," he told her in a gentle voice.

<hr />

THE TEAM MEETING was called in a conference room rather than the locker room. Katella had picked up some sandwiches from a nearby deli, with fruit and a variety of soft drinks. Besides the two assistant coaches, the goalie coach, and Cherney, the only other people allowed in the conference room were the players. Katella and Harper also took seats in the back.

Once everyone had some food, Seraphina walked up to the front, feeling more nervous than she had since taking control of the team. Even her first meeting with them where Alec called her out on her ignorance did not make her feel like this. Her hands were clammy, her heart raced in her chest and pounded against her ribs, her mouth was suddenly dry despite the entire water bottle she drank before walking in here.

When she caught eyes with Brandon, who sat in front, he gave her a look that said, *Relax. You've got this.*

Seraphina took a deep breath and glanced out at her team as a whole. Her heart continued to jackhammer against her chest, and she was struck with the feeling that she had somehow let these players down, like she had made a selfish decision that put her own needs before the team's. And then her eyes found Brandon's once more and those thoughts completely vanished from her head. Yes, she made a selfish choice. She chose to give into temptation after holding back for a year and a half. But that didn't make her a bad person. And, she had enough faith in her team that they would understand.

"Thank you guys so much for coming to this impromptu meeting," she began, interlacing her fingers together and pacing around the room. She wished there was a podium to hold onto because she never knew what to do with her hands. "I know it was relatively last minute." She crossed her arms over her chest. "As I know you know, Phil Bambridge is a dick." The team laughed. "But now, he's reached out proposing a trade. In exchange for Brandon Thorpe, he's willing to give us Avery, Duke, and Thompson."

The team got silent. Seraphina held her breath. She was aware what a tempting trade that was. Yes, she knew Thorpe was the best goalie in the league but games couldn't be won without goals.

"I, of course, said no," she continued. "There's no way I'm letting Bambridge take the best goalie in the league. I also have confidence that we'll get our scoring from all of you. I expect secondary scoring from our defense to our third and fourth lines. We're going to have to work our asses off but it'll be worth it, I promise you." Seraphina crossed her arms over her chest and turned around, pacing in the opposite direction.

"Tomorrow, I will be holding a press conference, coming out with the fact that Bambridge is blackmailing me. I don't plan to go into detail but I got some great advice from Drew Stefano and when I spoke with my lawyer, she agreed that the best way to combat blackmail is to tell the world the truth. Acknowledging what is happening takes power away. I'm telling you all of this because I want you to know that it's going to be a lot harder from here on out. Not that playing the sport and kicking ass isn't hard in the first place. But your manager and owner is a female who gets emotional and has feelings and a period and a vagina, and men don't know how to react to things they don't understand. And let me tell you, Phil Bambridge does not know how to talk to someone with a vagina.

"I guess what I'm trying to say is don't let them get in your heads. We're so close, I'm sure you can almost taste it. So let's keep going. Listen to Cherney and Anderson and Fasth. Listen to your coaches. When you go home, forget about hockey and hang out with your kids or your significant others or your friends. Don't fight for me or for Kat or for anyone else except for yourself and your teammates." She stopped pacing and perked her brows. "Do you have any questions?"

When no one raised their hands, she nodded. "Okay," she said. "I have the press conference set for tomorrow. Like I said, it's not mandatory to attend. Thank you guys so much for coming. If you have any questions at all, my door is always open."

The players filed out, leaving Seraphina, Katella, and Brandon by themselves. Negan threw Katella a look over his shoulder, almost as if to say, *I'll catch you later* and she winked in return.

Seraphina felt her insides warm at the exchange. Her sister was finally happy. She was making it work with a Gulls player, and she had a lot worse history than Seraphina did when it came to being with players. Maybe the media perceived Seraphina as inept, but they thought Katella was nothing short of a puck slut. And somehow, she got through it. She was happy. And if anyone called her that, she was certain Negan would defend Katella – if she needed the defending in the first place. Katella was apt at taking care of herself.

"You're awesome, Sera," Katella said, turning to her sister. "I'm so proud of you." Her gaze flickered over to Brandon before looking back at Seraphina. "I'm so happy for you as well. I'm glad you finally took that step."

Seraphina laughed but didn't say anything.

Katella glanced at Brandon. "You don't know it, but I've

been telling her to get with you since she took over the team," Katella pointed out. "So, you know, you're welcome."

Brandon laughed and Seraphina blushed.

"Where would we be without you, Kat?" she asked.

Chapter 25

"ARE YOU SURE ABOUT THIS?" Seraphina asked, cocking her head up to look at Brandon. "No one knows why we called this press conference. We can go out and tell them about us. We can go out and tell them we're excited because we're going to play-offs. We could tell them-"

"Sera," he said in a gentle voice, cupping her cheek with his palm. "It's okay. I want to do this."

Seraphina clenched her jaw. For some reason, she felt like crying, which didn't make any sense. She bit the inside of her bottom lip, hoping this would keep the tears at bay. She didn't want to cry in front of him. Not right now. Not when he needed her to be strong for him – whether he realized it or not.

"But everything you sacrificed," she pushed on. "Everything your mom and your sister sacrificed so you could make it this far in your career. It would be for nothing."

Brandon gave her a look. "Sera, we're making playoffs," he pointed out. "We have the chance to win the Cup this season before Petrov retires, before I-" He pushed his brows up. "We can do this. You've always had faith in me, and even after our worst season ever, we came back and we can have our best season on the books. Because of you. Not anyone else. Not even your grandfather. But because of *you*."

Seraphina nodded and pressed her lips together. She took a deep breath and glanced down at the notecards in her hands.

"Ready?" she asked him, looking up.

He nodded. "Absolutely."

From there, Seraphina and Brandon walked out from the club entrance of Sea Side Ice Palace. They weren't holding hands but they remained close together. When they reached the podium, the entire media immediately started to take pictures. Seraphina ignored the flashes as she usually did, but she was certain it bugged Brandon to a degree because he wasn't used to it. Even all the pictures taken during games were easy to ignore, and those done at fan events weren't this overwhelming. Seraphina stood in front of the podium, Brandon stood behind her, like a protective guardian angel.

"Thank you," she said into the microphone. The media quieted instantly and Seraphina had to bite back a smile. This was too easy. "I'd like to thank you all for coming. I'm sure you have questions based on Harper Crawford's article yesterday and you'll get to ask those in a little bit. However, I do want to come out and address you directly because I feel we've had a sort of love-hate relationship the past couple of years where you love to hate me. And, quite frankly, I'm sick of it and I'm sick of taking it.

"I'm sick of showing up to work early and leaving work late and rather than write about my work ethic, you're wondering if I'm starving myself to stay thin. I'm sick of making amazing pickups and good trades in the off-season and all you care about is whether or not my breasts are real. I'm sick of the fact that three NHL GM's are former hockey players with no actual college degree and yet I'm being questioned about whether I know the difference between a player's goals and a player's points.

"It doesn't matter that I majored in business and graduated

with honors from a university. It doesn't matter that my grandfather, a man you admired and respected, gave me the team because he thought I could do it. My grandfather, by the way, wasn't a former hockey player or a college graduate. He wasn't even from Canada. He never put on a pair of skates. But I guess since he's a white man with money, that makes him okay. That makes him worth respecting."

Seraphina rolled her eyes, a blatant show of defiance, taking everyone by surprise. Cameras flashed.

"You have written more articles about my sister like she's the star of some kind of soap opera," Seraphina continued. "Who she's dating, who she's sleeping with, how Matt Peters' career went down the drain since breaking up, how it's been better since being back with the team... You're so mean that you can't even keep up with your own headlines. You contradict yourself so much that I have no idea where you're getting your material from.

"Instead of writing about Dimitri Petrov's amazing point streak for a forty-two-year-old player, you write about his ex-wife kicking him out of the house," Seraphina said. "Instead of writing about Alec Schumacher's scholarship he created himself, you write about the fact that he might be gay because he suddenly stopped dating Gulls Girls. Instead of focusing on the team as a whole, you pick and choose players in order to sell your papers. And I get it. That's your job. I can respect that. But it's my job to protect my players. I can't control what you write, especially when you have someone like Phil Bambridge completely feeding you guys bullshit information."

There was a gasp in the crowd.

"Oh, I'm sorry," Seraphina said with a snarl. "Did I swear? Was that unladylike within the boundaries of the sport of hockey? I don't care. If I want to wear skinny jeans and a Batman belt, I'm going to wear that. I don't care what you write about me anymore. You're looking like idiots when you focus on my appearance rather than the fact that Brandon Thorpe's save percentage is 0.945, the highest in the league or the fact that Dimitri Petrov has thirty-seven goals. Or the fact that there's a damn good chance we're going to make playoffs for the first time in history.

"So, I'm letting you know, from here on out, I'm not going to play your stupid games. You can believe whatever you want to believe. If you're going to believe a man trying to stir things up because his lackluster team seems more preoccupied with partying in Vegas than they do with winning hockey games, by all means, go for it. I shouldn't have to remind you that this is the same man who got arrested on multiple occasions for sexually assaulting different women he quickly paid off to keep their mouths shut. And considering I am the only female GM, considering I have one of the best teams in the NHL, it's no surprise that Phil Bambridge sees me and The Gulls as a threat. It's why he's trying to blackmail me into trading away Brandon Thorpe. It's why he's trying to insinuate that I engage in inappropriate relationships with my team. I guess he's one of those guys who doesn't understand what the word no truly means. And God forbid he does, it can't possibly be because he's a guy I don't want to be around or engage in business with, it's because I'm a lesbian or some other reason." She paused. "And here I thought only privileged men could act professional and refrain from not acting on their emotions."

The media chuckled and Seraphina rolled her eyes.

"I guess what I'm trying to say is, let me do my job and you do yours," Seraphina said. "I won't be taking questions today. I just wanted to call this press conference in order to clarify a few points and ensure everyone was on the same page. Thank you for coming out here and for your time."

With that, she took a step back and Brandon gave her a small grin. It was a grin that carried a secret and he managed to nudge her with his shoulder in a subtle way, where nobody else noticed it. They walked back into the building among journalists shouting out questions and Harper smirking as she wrote down notes in her notebook.

Seraphina didn't care. Once they were away from the spectators, from the onlookers and gossips, Seraphina grabbed Brandon's hand and led him to the nearby elevators.

"That was amazing," he murmured as she pressed the up button. She smiled at him and he kissed the top of her head. "I am so proud of you."

"This just means we have to be really careful, Brandon," Seraphina said. "I have no idea if Bambridge is going to release the pictures or not. Regardless, we have to make sure you and I don't get caught. I would be forced to either trade you, have you retire, or give the team to someone else. I know my uncles want any reason to get their hands on this team, especially since we're making playoffs."

"This team will not belong to your uncles," Brandon promised her, squeezing her hand for emphasis. It was clear in the look he was giving her that he wanted to go more but understood that there were cameras in the elevator and it wouldn't be the smartest thing to do, especially if they were trying to stay under the radar. "I would retire first before I ever let that happen."

"Good, because they would ruin you guys, let me tell you," Seraphina said. The elevator doors slid open, and Seraphina led Brandon out. The offices were completely empty. Unless there was a scheduled game, Seraphina did not require anyone to work on Sunday.

When they reached her office, Seraphina closed the door behind them and drew the blinds. Brandon perked his brow, clearly surprised. "What's going on?" he asked. "You never close your office door."

"Yeah, well technically, I'm not working," she said, stepping into his arms. "We're going to make playoffs, Mr. Thorpe. For the first time in your career, you're going to make playoffs. How do you feel right now?"

"Honestly?" he asked, gently perking his brows. Seraphina nodded. "I don't give a shit about that. I mean, it's awesome and I'm stoked. I think we can really be a competitive team. But I'm more concerned about you and me. I'm really excited about that more than anything else."

Seraphina rolled her eyes. "You are such a romantic," she said.

Brandon shrugged. "I guess you just bring it out in me," he told her.

"Oh, so it's my fault?" she asked.

He nodded. "Totally your fault," he said, pulling her into a kiss. "So, tell me how this is going to work."

"What?" Seraphina asked.

"You and me," he said. "I know we're supposed to be careful but does that mean we can't date at all? No more brunch at the beach? No more holding your hand as we walk down the boardwalk?"

"I don't know," Seraphina said. "It wouldn't surprise me in the slightest if Bambridge sends out a PI just to try and get further proof that you and I are an item. But I promised myself I wouldn't make decisions based on how others perceive me. I can't live in fear of that and you shouldn't either."

"So what should we do, then?" he asked, leaning towards her so his lips were a ghost's breath away from hers.

"Well, for starters, you can kiss me," she told him slowly, her eyes never leaving his. "And from there, we'll take things day by day and see where are in a few months. All I know is that you're the one I want to be with at the end of the day, Brandon. Not anyone else. You are all that matters to me."

He smiled – a beaming smile that lit up his entire face and took her breath away – and kissed her once more.

Want to know when Book 4 comes out?

Positives & Penalties: Book 4 in the Slapshot Series will be released August 25, 2017. Preorder it now for 99 pennies - but only for a limited time!

Want updates on when my latest book comes out, exclusive giveaways, and free stuff? Sign up for my newsletter here!

Did You Like Lip Locks & Blocked Shots?

As an author, the best thing a reader can do is leave an honest review. I love gathering feedback because it shows me you care and it helps me be a better writer. If you have the time, I'd greatly appreciate any feedback you can give me. Thank you!

Acknowledgments

The Anaheim Ducks because they're my team no matter what - especially the team from 2011. My inaugural season. ;)

My family

My friends

The work squad

Susan H. & Becky for your amazing edits and suggestions! My writing is better because of you!

Susanna Lynn, for your beautiful cover. It's amazing and stunning and perfect!

Thank you to my readers who have fallen in love with this series, with hockey, and with the amazing players. I write for YOU!

Frank & Kylee, Josh & Jacob, for your continued love, support, and understanding

Also by Heather C. Myers

The Slapshot Series: A Sports Romance

Blood on the Rocks, Snapshot Prequel, Book 1 Her grandfather's murdered and she's suddenly thrust with the responsibility of owning and managing a national hockey team. That, and she decides to solve the murder herself.

Grace on the Rocks, Slapshot Prequel, Book 2 A chance encounter at the beach causes sparks to fly...

Charm on the Rocks, Slapshot Prequel Book 3 When you know it's wrong but it feels so right

The Slapshot Prequel Box Set

Exes & Goals, Book 1 of the Slapshot Series Most people have no regrets. She has one.

Black Eyes & Blue Lines, **Book 2 of the Slapshot Series** He drives her crazy - and not in a good way. But she can't get him out of her head.

Lip Locks & Blocked Shots, **Book 3 of the Slapshot Series** He's the last person she should fall in love with and the only one that ever stood a chance.

Also by Heather C. Myers

Modern Jane Austen Retellings

Four Sides of a Triangle Matchmaking is supposed to be easy. But Madeline is going to learn that love can't be planned when she starts to fall for the last person she ever thought she would, who also happens to be the man her best friend claims to love as well.

Stubborn Marion is a die-hard USC fan. Aiden goes to UCLA Law School. If only college rivalries were the worst of their problems. They say opposites attract. Well, some crash into each other.

Also by Heather C. Myers

New Adult Contemporary Romance

Save the Date As daughter of a man in charge of the CIA, Gemma knew her father was overprotective. She just never thought he would assign a man she couldn't stand to be her bodyguard under the rouse of a fake marriage.

On Tour with the Rockstar Holly Dunn didn't know that when she began studying at a rock concert, the lead singer would call her out on it. Tommy Stark didn't know he'd be intrigued by her odd sort of ways, which was why hew invited her to go on tour with him.

Foolish Games She was everything he didn't want in a woman and everything he couldn't resist. She thought he was arrogant on top of other things.

Falling Over You She wasn't supposed to see him, hear him, or feel him because he was dead - a ghost. She wasn't supposed to fall in love with him because she was engaged.

Hollywood Snowfall It's getting cold in Hollywood, so cold, there's a good chance the City of Angels will finally get snow.

Also by Heather C. Myers

Dark Romance

A Beauty Dark & Deadly He's the most beautiful monster she's even seen

A Reputation Dark & Deadly Logan Jeffrey has a reputation

Also by Heather C. Myers

Young Adult Novels

<u>Trainwreck</u> Detention is not the place where you're supposed to meet your next boyfriend, especially when he's Asher Boyd, known pothead and occasional criminal. But he makes good girl Sadie Brown feel something she hasn't really felt before - extraordinary.

Also by Heather C. Myers

Science Fiction/Fantasy

Battlefield Just because they were, quite literally, made for each other didn't mean they had to actually get along.

Made in United States
Orlando, FL
17 January 2024

42625663R20108